Apathy and Atrophy

BY

T.C.S. Miller

Copyright ©
2024 T.C.S. Miller
All Rights Reserved.

Chapter 1

"Life is the art of the possible—luckily I know everything is just that"! As this triumphant aphorism emerged from the café, so too did the gregarious figure of Max pouring as he did, out of the row of low-slung terraced houses like oil from a newly tapped drum. Behind him, and with a knowing smile and wave, Anna retracted, telescopically, into her West London flat share. Whenever leaving this woman's abode Max always wondered whether the genteel Anna, the personification of soft power, would ever give into herself and become the crook she was always meant to be. They were an interesting pair; not so much two sides of the same coin as two antlers growing from the same skull only now beginning to cut through life's gorse differently.

It was with this thought passed that Max started towards the river.

He trotted past the various stripped-down coffee shops, the peak of the globalised world's civilisation and wondered why him, why now? What gave him, what he'd decided he so clearly had, the transformative spark that turned him from an adolescent drifter into an adult striver; for not six months ago there hadn't been this possibility, or, indeed, its corresponding impossibility, but rather a reality or an unreality. Education, tertiary inclusive, which to some had been an exercise in compression of the soul had, for him, been a boys-own tale of going with the flow. Like most things in life the end had been decided on by the beginning, not that he was aware of this at the time, and thus lashings, strengthened by the muddying coagulation of adventure, had bounded him buoyant regardless of the river's lurching. Others, those who had been somewhat overwhelmed by the mould, had been lost and found like panned gold; sprinklings of circumstance in an otherwise told story. This impermanence rendered these others merely the colourings of memorial shards, who left to their own devices formed the very sand that kept the body flowing—not that they knew it at the time either.

As he continued down the road, however, Max's thoughts turned to what lay ahead of him that evening. It was March, and the poker game above the Dog and Duck in Fulham was now a weekly occurrence. He and his friends had picked the location for the country pub cosiness of its upstairs, which rendered it the black dog of the riverside gastropubs. It had been a favourite since their mid-teens, and so under the ever-tightening noose of drinking laws and gentrification, the boys had stayed loyal to the establishment's stained, dark-wooded innards. Not, of course, in some romantic desire for community, permanence or indeed loyalty, nor ostensibly a desire to embrace a perceived past to brace for the future—these were not men of old. Really, it had been its easy location and the alternating flows of other loose social groups through the boozer's weeping walls.

"But back to Anna," Max thought, "What now separated her from Max?" The question perplexed him. "Maybe she just stayed on the river,"

While others of his age—but no one he knew—might see spectres of their past or even future while walking down a road like this, Max saw characters instead. He saw the florist, he saw the butcher, and he saw the sales assistant, but it was the latter that held his attention. He saw the role and not the person. Max's recent réalisation—that the suppression of conscience was the key to success—had delineated his already cartoonish picture of the world into a caricatural canvas of personality traits. Á la Marinetti Max saw the technicolours linked by currents in all their writhing beauty; their driving and tugging seemed like great movements relative to the frittering of the organisms he used to stare at under a microscope. He felt powerful. The fact Max felt he could see all of this and mirror it delighted him, and as the potentialities formed in his head he rearranged them repeatedly, reforming the world in front of his very eyes. This newly added intellectual dimension to his masturbation allowed Max to create and solve these Rubik's cubes at will. Each of these then became an all-rationalising lantern for each step into the unknown, they worked like cameras, individually set, able to record with full narrative control.

So, it was with this head full of promise that Max passed the vestiges of others' decisions. He passed entire bodies of thought, questions and conclusions infinitesimal in their extent, hamstrung by his self-deified reality juggling. Askew maybe, but constantly in motion, like a soundscape he set the tone.

*

Max arrived at the place and ordered a couple of pints, and sat himself in the centre of the room, waiting for his friends. The landlord served him, neither knew one another's name, while Max looked out over the Thames. The overcast day had now thinned to a sky like crinkled tin foil, thickly spread, with jagged light shining through the newly broken cloud. The river was still and opaque and flanked by cold mud followed by a wall on each side. Hammersmith was bleak. While on Max's side this wall formed part of the well-defined boundary between curated civility and the stygian natural world, on the other it was merely abutted by a thick wood. Over there dog walkers and runners, trying to catch the last gasps of the weekend, were short-changed with the immateriality of the coming days. March, the transitory month, was wearing on and wearing down. A rebirth was needed. But a rebirth to what? The future wasn't set, of course, but it was predictable.

"The great wheels of economy and society still turn and look … look at all they give us,"

Max's mind trailed off as he took a deep slurp of ale. He kept drinking, further lining his stomach with the bitterness of acceptance, and soon was down to little enough beer to address others confidently without spillage. Wheeling slowly, to prepare himself, he turned to one of the regulars most amenable to conversation, but as he did so saw his pals amble in—and he thanked God.

Sharpened and shaking he and his friends hugged and slapped their way through the customary greetings—Max had effortlessly slipped into himself. Here he had an identity so fixed that it was a place and a sanctuary in this barren land of possibility. Where others might be buffeted by the storm Max and his friends were an amorphous organism reforming themselves over and over again, but never separating, as they made their way through life. Now, more exposed than ever, as the cathedral they'd occupied for so long crumbled and fissured against the elements, they retreated and further and huddled closer on their island against the unknown. Billy, Harry, Nick and Paul, the game's regulars, were a mismatch of differing degrees of eccentricity—although they'd moved beyond such puerile jabbings—yet continuous in their affronting ease. Together they nodded to the barman and proceeded upstairs to open the room and get everything set up. What followed was not a fair division of labour, but a fair division of duty. Thus the evening began, and as they rolodexed through the catching-up-small talk, each basked in its familiarity.

The first three pints and however-many-hands passed unremarkably, but on jars four and five the conversation heated up with Nick ranting on about the girl he was sleeping with. On the sixth, however, the mood turned more introspective and Paul and Billy kept playing but dealt themselves out of the conversation. This went unremarked upon and the two were left to their silence by the rest's unutterable pining for their chosen stability; the regular seemed enticing to those in thrall to it, yet comparison was dangerous. None were under the daily cracking whip of necessity, and all were driven enough, the only difference was what they wanted the rest of their lives to be. For these were the early days—each was at a different place in their realisation that the key to Snakes and Ladders is merely how hard you roll the dice.

Cards, beer and cigarette breaks passed as the afternoon rolled into evening and dinner orders were put in at the bar; as the breaks grew longer, and the cigarettes smoked progressively more pensively, hands became more irregular and adult play degenerated to real play; jabbing chips and wagged forks rose and spurted; the table was slammed and bumped under and atop with exclamations as each boy wormed his way backwards and forwards in ritualistic undulation. Eventually, repletion was achieved and its purchase in their heads had them slumped, one by one, backwards, in sweated relaxation. The honesty of earlier was straw-manned and contorted into wry throwaways that ham-fistedly, served to tie up the evening's loose ends. Finally, as the ever-fraying tapestry was re-rationalised and re-established each of the men felt the nagging pull of retreat into their own lives. The unerring cycle of rebirth morphed the set of dowdy strays into a pack of animals each a-quiver with ebullience, and their waltzing and prancing out into the night bore them to their respective homes like warm butter slaking dry toast—each leaving Max's mind—interludes off a stage.

Max opted for a cab to take him home and, waving one down with a pleasurable calm, directed the driver to his newly rented flat. Once inside he navigated the hermaphroditic array of education and life detritus and after a thorough evening routine, got into bed and fell asleep. In the night, however, his fears were on him. He dreamed he was running through this grey city head stooped and neck warped like Quasimodo. In pursuit were the Police. Officers chased him down alleys, cut off exits in cars and predicted his next move from helicopters. The inflaming beam of a spotlight was utterly implacable and determined to catch him like a deer in the dark, and with each stride, jump and dodge his animus was depleted and his vigour drained. Little by little Max's straining movements were numbed into a pendulous swing and, empty now, he may as well have been running in a vacuum. All that remained then was a searing corporeal pain as if his blood had been replaced with poison and his organs rendered lifeless, only fit to be removed.

Chapter 2

Max gasped awake and lay, immobile, staring at his ceiling and the opposite bedroom wall. Flashes of the dream still burned in his head but mercifully most had been lost to the well of his subconsciousness. The hangover and disturbed night's sleep had rendered Max's body limp from the resulting nocturnal thrashings. These nightmares weren't uncommon and although they usually shared similar themes, it was their visceral nature that rendered Max unable to dispel the haze they left him in the morning after.

Luckily, however, as he wasn't working today (freelancing had its perks) Max was able to slowly wrap a dressing gown around himself and gingerly descend the varnished wooden steps to begin a fry-up. Netflix went on and content blared. He filled a pan with the brown greasy mess that sustained him—sausages, bacon, mushroom and baked beans—while carefully scrambling the eggs in a second receptacle. Mayonnaise and brown sauce topped the life-giving medley and he sat letting the sitcom calm his mind. Familiar lines and dancing jingles were a balm to him, like waves satiating the sand of a beach. Yet just as tides deconstruct their picturesque accompaniment, the repetition of yet another morning ordered and structured into nothing tugged away at Max.

"Why do I, a man with the world at my feet, live such a humdrum life," he mused to himself. "Well, I have allowed it to be so," he retorted, "I have let myself drift to this place, this slow current of the meandering river. I am an impotent, a fool, who am I to deny that? I can't! Yet I have known only this, that which I am now? How can this be, how I can be here!"

Here, overwhelmed by his megalomania, Max slumped down and passed out.

*

Max woke again, now back in his bed, with the thick dressing gown wrapped uncomfortably around his clammy body. He was still boyish, manliness had been rather irregularly gifted, and a bit of a waif. All through his figure was a slight asymmetry that lent him a striking and somewhat androgynous presence. His features were individual, but in keeping with everything else, discordant when taken together. Yet it was this higgledy-piggledy assemblage that'd meant he always felt more than the sum of his parts; for whatever made "him" up others seemed to add something too. This something was best seen in the singular way those around him seemed to interact with him. There was always an accepted distance, deferential in some cases—it was odd but worked in his favour, so he chose not to think about it. His softness had currency too. Again, he rarely thought of it, but his body seemed stuck on the boundary of adulthood only just tearing through first youth. Yes, all was odd, but all seemed to work in his favour, that was his feeling.

Max considered all of this and slowly his whimsically indulgent self-adulation began to crystallise into an idea. He went to his laptop typed a few names into Wikipedia and scrolled to their personal life section. Most had higher educational achievements than him and all seemed to have some sort of story that explained their place in the world at the time of writing. After perusing multiple bios, and getting their feel, Max began to see these justifying narratives as poles thrust into desert sands, that formed an ostensibly followable path through the arid landscape of life. It was the presumed sense of the unmentioned, bone-dry, rest of the picture that both intrigued and resonated with him.

"I feel something stirring within, something knurled, deep within my innards, it writhes and lurks. But never mind, I will turn my life into these bullet points, I will compartmentalise my experiences, into these blocks of singular identities, they will be alien, but they will be mine to manipulate."

Max now saw the cascades of data everywhere he looked, each only defined by whichever structuring brackets he chose to apply—why should he not reflect this in his own construction? He took off his dressing gown and looked at his now naked body in the mirror, surveying each of his supposed imperfections, and realised the jutting angles and malformations he saw were only those he had determined as relevant today. He turned his head slowly from side to side,

"These features of mine are mine to change; from one to the other I can expand or contract them, I can make them and unmake them; and even then, these are only that which I have deemed features"!

He concentrated like this for some time and gradually the room itself began to lose stability. Tracers appeared in his eyes like dying stars presenting the remnants of a lost reality.

Vertices began to repeat themselves laying down like the sleepers of reptilian train tracks making their way across the lens. Blank walls shimmed with minute crawling movements that now covered them and coloured themselves with ever longer exposures.

Distressed by this vision and hyperventilating Max plunged back into his laptop. His greasy hands dirtied the pristine keys and he rapidly began to create his own page. Thundering through the facts. Max only slowed once he'd completed his twined cot, and began to plot his river. But unlike the others, he decided he would carve the desert up with his journey.

"I won't be stopped by the shifting sands, instead I will atrophy the landscape and dig down and dig deep; I will forge the sand into glass and then dig down until my pick hits the cold prehistoric rock below; I'll flood the ravine and force water down it, smoothing the cut first to a groove and then to a bed; the river will flow thick and fast so as to create a feature of time immemorial and to be kept pure and clean; and as it grows in size and strength it will be able to break through the relief, rather than abiding by its undulations and directions; I will become the rationalising force of the land bending which is to become mine own!"

He, the arbiter, everyone else the arbitrated, it was possible—the dynamic could be brought to life.

"But can I really permanently freeze the landscape or will this become an ever-executing conviction?" Max paused, "But surely the glass would be cracked and eventually broken. The only constant may be change but so too is my change constant."

These pithy witticisms began to tumble out of him.

"How can too many cooks spoil the broth and many hands make light work," he asked himself. "Well of course people just apply whichever best suits the situation, it was all merely narrative creation – it was clear: the only truth was the paradox of both being beliefs fundamental to the human condition. In which case I must be doing the right thing as I'm dealing with this eternal paradox, and my change is the only constant response."

His desires, and his reasons for those desires, were becoming repetitions of one another. Each's nature was the nature of the other. His history, human history—he bent it all back on itself. That, which for as long as he'd lived, had seemed like the tumbling of a stained corpse, flat, out in front of itself, he now began to form into a sphere. This singularity, eternal, the alpha and omega, was made of every possible iteration of experience understood in its fullest form. Each of these circles fitted snugly together magnetised by one another's presence as realisation begot realisation. Soon the ball began to shine. Its brilliance filled the void, surrounding it until it obliterated all of the nothing outside of its self-perpetuating existence. Now sweating, Max tapped out the final references at the bottom of his page and collapsed onto his desk.

*

Again he awoke, now in the early evening. The sun was being swallowed by the clouds but Max was unable to look at what he'd done—again he struggled to the shower, washed and emerged in a crisp pair of boxers—still averted from his antediluvian actions he slowly picked up the bits and bobs that littered his flat, dusted, hoovered, wiped, adjusted; and was eventually able to stand comfortably in his brochure ready home. Suddenly starving, Max pulled together a sandwich and washed it down with a drink all the while warily eyeing his now cooled laptop. With these staccato actions completed and his heart pounding so hard it jangled his ribs, he sat down in front of his laptop and investigated what exactly he'd done.

Max skimmed the page five times, picking up snippets here and there, before he settled into a reading pace. In an effort to grab the bull by the horns and avoid a possible rising panic attack, he opened "Early Life" and read. Unsurprisingly, he surmised, it bore no relation to the last twenty or so years of his life. It was that which the others were—artificial predictors of success—the ramp would jettison him into the stratosphere. There was a passion project directing emotional trauma, some minor displacement and most importantly evidence of an early start. "After all," he said to himself, "Our heroes are born not made." Now he was able to settle back in his chair and ponder what exactly to do next. This Icebreaker he'd created, while an exploratory vessel, was still answerable to the winds and tides of whatever came next. The possibilities were endless really, and under his new moniker *Ahriman* he could spark the fires that forged his bucket for putting them out—it was brilliant.

Chapter 3

Buoyed by the action taken, Max called up Anna and asked if she was free that evening. He pictured her with her customary straight bob and minimalist glasses and looked forward to the feigned derision and purring delight of her hiding her affection for him. She was a busy woman but had made time for him at such short notice before, and, he presumed, was secretly thankful for his throwing a line into the ever-enveloping pit of her career. This was backed with some proof, but undoubtedly relied in part on the compartmentalised vision of each other's life they presented to one another,

"I the svelte figure of polymathic potential and her the Mistress of the Universe," he mused to himself.

Together they formed a good pair and so when they, as they occasionally did, bumped into one another at the pub, they could keep up their fronted flirtation and enjoy the room melt away around their perfect—if a little obvious—tryst. They'd met years ago, of course, during school, Max vaguely recollected.

Mercifully Anna picked up after only a few rings and after some flirtatious pressing agreed to meet round the corner for a late dinner. The dinner was important he felt.

They had been in one another's sexual pickings for so long that the hollowness of the honest emotion they had for one another needed to be obfuscated by some standard of behaviour. Theirs wasn't a *will they won't they*, relationship but rather a, *they will until they won't*.

"Eventually we'll move on from this bollocks, I suppose," Max mused to himself, "But where it takes me before that happens … well I suppose that is hardly any of my business."

Later, in an efficient little Italian pizzeria, they danced the alcohol-drenched fairy-tale flirtation. The coos, the eyebrows and the intakes of breath were individually perfunctory beats, together undulating guiding an assumed audience. The conversation had some perks, however, as both had a myriad of ridiculousness refusing to leave their lives. For Anna it was the blatant inefficiency of the startup she was working for—the pitching and yawing of this newly built boat, in the yet-to-be-defined waters of her sector, was becoming a breeding ground for the sort of bureaucratic fuckery she'd been raised to have a predilection against. After all, she was pugnacious, in the blonde, privately educated way, a clear product of the London day school scene. On this, frankly passé, point, Max really began to focus on her.

Anna had a fantastic ability, though rarely used now, to lead one to certain conclusions and he couldn't help but respect it. There was still a sense, an intuition which, though it needed nurturing, left him in boyish wonderment at the sight of her.

*

With the final act agreed on, conversation languished and they swiftly walked back to Max's flat, past packed-up seats and closed doors. The parties had moved inside to be safe from the darkness leaving those stealing through the night a clear path to their sordid destinations. Streets devoid of people as much as they were devoid of meaning, no longer the arteriole walls of a pumping, vibrant body, they were now mere concrete sewers charged down by the unappreciative uncaring inhabitants of an ever more disjointed world. Walking through the night superficialities abounded as people simply accepted their own inevitable dislocation from all that once was—the past is a foreign country as they say. British suicidality, long documented by those on the continent, had swelled to terrifying proportions in recent years and the sky had long been overcast, for decades maybe, but now the city's lights were going out, one by one, in acquiesce to this ghoulish wilting.

Returned, they tugged at each other's clothes with frisky abandon, and grazed each other's lips. They cut away at their respective refinements with clawing hands and driving chins, revealing the taut flesh of their coiling bodies. Clarified by voyeurism, thrusts and grabs—definite movements, softened one another and soon each in their own way became pliant to the other's will. Sex, once an act individual construction was now a plethora of psychologised power dynamics. The beast with two backs had long since died leaving a descriptive automaton guarding the route to pleasure. Like a piston Max's function defined his form and he was soon directionally thrusting like a nodding donkey, vying for a gushing. Anna, a vision of pillowed royalty, was pressed against the wall like a tipped-over mannequin head turned and mouth silently agape observing the proceedings in a parallel mirror.

Now naked and aiming to keep it fresh they walked into the kitchen, Anna was bent over another surface—and so the farce continued. An hour later Max was drenched in sweat and the pair were sitting opposite one another drinking beers under the harsh kitchen light. Max combed his bedraggled hair back over his ears with his hand while Anna neatly smoothed hers back into a tight ponytail. They were broken before one another and unwound with drinks and cigarettes; their heads hung and their pupils retreated slightly into their eyes. Each's numbed vulnerability caused the befuddled explanation of thought-away emotions and glimpses of inner yearnings. As they sat together, almost holding hands, the world outside this room, their sanctuary, fell away leaving them in fear of the void outside. Under that bright light of revelation, their suppleness faded, and imperfections rose to the forefront, their bodies aged beyond their years and vivacity gave way, a resignation to the ever-deepening trenches that defined their lives. Their erotic flustering's fading was replaced by blotchy rosacea and directed down to over-drawn necks and lumping flesh. Now accustomed to the deconstructed beauty of one another, wryness returned and their drinks went down quicker. Finally, with events now tied up, the pair rose stiffly and plodded upstairs each only interrupting the other's ascent with a cheeky slap of the bum.

Early the next morning they awoke together, and Max, shrivelling, looked to the rather more elegant figure of Anna and said his goodbyes. She'd had her cosmetics in a bathroom cupboard for as long as he'd lived in the flat and after a final round last night had attended to her evening routine, slept, woke up, performed her morning routine, and was to return to hers for a quick change before heading to the office. And again, Max was alone and, wrenched from his slumber, was in a drowsy limbo. As he began to doze he was wrapped up by another dream. This time he was the lone white man at an African tribe's festival. Details were sparse other than a large fire, bright colours, and ritualised actions. Without waking Max began to be pulled towards the fire, soon finding himself inside the circle of prancing worshippers. He looked deep into the curling flames and charcoaling wood. Suddenly he began to suffocate. His breath wasn't being stolen from him, rather all that allowed him to breathe was being removed. He could feel his physical form being pulled away from him, he looked down at his open palms and vascular arms and watched as they began to blur and crease, the veins wriggling away like worms off hot metal. Soon he was left with only the hint of pigment, an illusion of humanity, and a face appeared in front of his with bright eyes and a huge smile. It uttered something with a provoking unkindness unheard by Max and as he fell further into himself, his vision was swallowed by the black hole of his soul.

*

Max started awake, panting, and wept with his face ground into the salted sheets. Curled like a baby, butting, trying to force the door of a closed womb, limbs utterly useless after his unconscious thrashing, he shuffled with his shoulders and hips—he was reduced to a wide-eyed reptilian, withered and frozen under the unblinking gaze of a watching hawk. The shivers of existential terror ran through him like herds of charging horses; they trampled his vain efforts to raise himself from the bed, their hooves pummelling him—a stoned unbeliever. Finally, in abject surrender to that which he could neither understand nor conceive of, he lay, uncomfortably on the unmade sheets that jabbed like spears into his length, a whimpering wreck.

Now convinced his invisible predator had moved its eye to other prey Max rose and looked at his bed and then at himself in the mirror.

"What am I," Max wondered?"

The vision of the decrepit that looked back at him had as little idea as he what there was to do, let alone to be. After enough of this introspection, to balm the burning ache inside his chest, Max set about cleaning this new mess.

Later—breakfasted—he switched to surveying that which was around him. This couldn't continue, Max knew it.

"More of the same, the same of more, whichever way around I arrange everything in front of me I return to the same emptiness. I suffer, I do, poor old me, I suffer from myself, I know this too. I know everything, yet I do nothing. I'm beyond shame, it must be said, for how can one feel shame when one is master of one's universe? Is shame a social construct, even? I'm not sure it matters, if enough people treat it as one, doesn't that mean it is one? After all, we do all walk through each other's values, treading on them unthinkingly. Yet I do have one option, one that would allow me to propel myself forward to excellence. I've even begun it, I suppose. Maybe then I may as well continue with it—I could go without to go within, become the sewer of my soul—I think. I say, I know, really I've already decided— *Ahriman* will carry me."

It was with this newfound satisfaction that Max narrowed his eyes, almost comically, and bobbed his head back and forth like a deflating buoy struggling to stay afloat.

Chapter 4

A week later Max had recovered himself from his self-induced mania. He was at his last ebb, and continuing felt like drawing blood from a stone. Since his decision, wherever he looked, he'd been crowded by the impersonal, as he saw it, that which was uninterested in him—a human. This degradation filled him just as his blood left him, and as this cycle slowly replaced him with something else, something alien, he would whisper to himself,
"I am human, I am man."
The torment ended on Saturday when a university friend invited him out for drinks. Thankful for this escape, Max got ready slowly that evening while an early dinner of stew simmered on the stove. Little by little he ironed out the creases of his wretched life and grew back into the vivacious young man he'd once been. Posturing and preening in front of the mirror he practised standing up straight, and then, leaning lightly back into his lower right shoulder, practised the slight coil that he felt framed his face best. Now in clean clothes, Max swaggered around his kitchen swigging a tin and giving his stew a few cursory stirs, revving himself up to his most social self—jokes were cracked to invisible fits

of laughter and, now jocular, he gobbled down his stew and headed out.

As he walked towards the pub from Kentish Town tube, Max enjoyed the encroaching buildings of North London and wound his way through the narrow streets like one smuggling himself away. On reaching the hole-in-the-wall establishment, Max paused for a second, caught his breath, and swung open the door expectantly. The pub was small, but the enclosed garden extended out like a wide alleyway thick with benches and unused heaters. Max ordered a pint at the bar and took a couple of sips as he craned his neck around the post. Alex was outside and Max wandered out to meet him, recognising some of the surrounding twenty-somethings through the mass of punters washed out from an afternoon of drinking. The pair embraced, and the stocky block that was Alex scratched his cheek against Max's. After Max had hugged those he knew, Alex introduced him to the unknowns. Max made the necessary greetings but stayed planted firmly with his friends so as to make the best of the night—the newbies were largely pleasant however and as the drinks went down everyone began to intermingle.

Shouting louder and louder above the rest, as the sky began to darken, was a friend of one of said newbies named Matt; a man of average height with a widow's peak and a chubby face. As his conversational gambits worsened those around him increasingly inched away antagonising his already spiky demeanour. As far as Max could gauge the man worked quite hard and wanted everybody to know that. Beyond that everything that came out his mouth seemed to be an effort to twist a conversation between two individuals into one about something general enough for him to shout platitudes about. Completely fed up after almost two hours of this drivel, the group—apart from Matt—decided to go to a bar. Matt was left in the loo, where he had been routinely going anyway, to sniff lines and harass strangers. It was on the way to the bar that Alex received a call, ending it, he turned and shouted,

"Sophie's meeting us at Pablo's," the crowd cheered.

"... Oh, she's great you'll love her," someone assured Max;

"Absolutely stunning as well," added another;

"Ed's fancied her for years," one of the girls shrieked and pointed at the rather luckless face of one of the men at the back of the group.

"She's so pretty, so, so pretty, it's unreal," continued the girl—"a little entranced herself," Max thought.

"I'll make sure you chat to her, don't worry, you'll love her, you really will!".

They all wandered towards Pablo's with Max assured of everyone's interest in himself and Sophie.

*

Sophie, the woman herself, walked in as the group was getting seated. She was tall and slim with a coquettish expression and dancing green eyes. Her greetings wafted over a cigarette and seemed to take the breath out of her listener's lungs only to replace it with her own. Max almost swooned as she slowly moved between those she knew generously gifting them with light kisses. When they finally faced one another Max's lower lip hung suspended between expressions, while his eyes softened with wonder. She too slowed, smiled with her perfectly angled lips and introduced herself. They sat together chatting away and Max introduced himself as working in the film industry and she in journalism.

Their conversation quickly began to tumble out with anecdotes, career issues, and the general chatter of two people finding more and more in common as their tones fell further and further into step. Max suggested a cigarette and they picked their way outside, aware of the others' eyes, lost to one another, far away from the spectators. They were truly a pair.

In the garden, Sophie mentioned an exhibition she was covering, and, in her mirth, she babbled about all there was to do.

"… Honestly, the amount we do to end up doing absolutely nothing, it's unbelievable! Anyway, who knows what's going on, I think I just want to be in London, I'm not sure anyone can honestly say they have more reason to be where they are in their lives than the accident of where they've drifted to. It's like being borne down a river and then let go of, where did you think we'd end up?"

With that, Sophie threw her arms up in the air and Max was left looking into the eyes of someone who could finally see into his. The conversation drifted away, and they were left facing one another, minds quieted under the care of one another's stares.

As their connection intensified their tones became hushed. With heavy eyelids and lingering palms the pair drew closer together.

"… Maybe I should have mentioned the handsome stranger I was hoping to meet here," Sophie whispered, and with that, finally, they kissed.

They were together for a long time, their lips found each other's again and again until, eventually, after sealing some covenant between them, Sophie explained she needed to leave. They parted as if a ribbon, sure of their re-joining one another. As Max watched her go everything he'd ever felt, apart from perfect contentment, was washed away. He had been baptised and born anew under the purifying deluge of their connection. Everything that was or would be fell away under her gaze and yet he was not left alone on some island; rather, he was elevated to some higher place, a part of some newfound continuum. Max stepped back into the wall and watched his breath curl up into the night sky. He smoked a cigarette slowly. The tobacco crackled in his mouth and transported him to a bonfire where, arms around Sophie, he was warmed regardless of the cold.

After a time spent basking in this newfound something, and indeed rather drunk, he wheeled around and wandered back inside. Overcome by an urge to be alone and enjoy his memory of the evening, Max said his goodbyes and, coat zipped up, headed back out into the street. He walked to the tube and, returning to Sophie, looked forward to calling her tomorrow.

Practically bounding and lost in the possibilities of future evenings with Sophie, Max turned a corner and walked straight into an inebriated Matt. Max bounced back, surprised but unhurt. Matt, on the other hand, sprawled back onto the pavement and hit his head with a sharp crack. Shocked, Max stood still not knowing what to do, but a grunting Matt raised himself off the ground to reveal a splatter of blood from where he'd landed. Max's gaze was distracted by this and so he missed Matt regaining his faculties and flaring his eyes. Suddenly the stocky drunk was on him pinning him to the ground and repeatedly punching him in the face while showering him in Stella-flavoured spittle. Max's hand reached back and found a brick behind his head. He brought it down on Matt's wound and his assailant howled in pain. Quickly extricating himself Max looked down at the now curled-up Matt and felt the weight of the brick in his palm. His mouth throbbed and he ran a parched tongue around his gums tasting blood. He smacked his lips together and still more blood oozed out and ran down each side of his chin; a tooth had come loose and he could feel it sitting behind his bottom teeth;

"Who the hell do you think you are, you gauche bastard? How the hell do you expect to be able to behave like that, to compete with someone like me? How dare you force me to reduce myself to your measly existence? How dare you, how dare you, how dare you?"

Max finished, swallowing some more blood. It was thick, metallic, and delicious. He closed his palm and imperiously regarded the wretched Matt, an ogre under the bounty hunter's blade. He could feel blood lining his innards and meeting the adrenaline filling his body. His shoulders rounded, his back widened, and without thinking he tightened his grip on the brick and stared coldly down at the pathetic, grovelling Matt, before bringing justice down onto his oh-so-inviting skull.

*

Max staggered back, torn from his cognisance, and looked down at his handiwork. He raised his hands to his face and, still holding the brick in his right hand, gave it to his left and thus revealed the unsullied handprint that broke the unremitting splattering of red which covered the already dusted brick. Before him was a skull cleaved in two by a fissure running from above to below the left eye. The remnants of the ball once held snugly within the socket were scattered over the pavement, washed out of their home by a flood of blood. So covered was the face that only the brilliant whites of his mouth's righthand occupants broke the sea of red. The rest of the limbs had been bundled around him by the spasming that had ensued after the strike.

Max was paralysed and could only look at what he'd done. His breath left him, everything fell away, and he was back on the island he knew so well except now he was there with company. Together they burned under the unyielding sun. The void he'd lived in for so long, that had once extended into the nether as an empty mass of burrow-able matter to hide in, now disappeared. Everything, now, was defined by the light. There was nothing outside of it, its beams served as walls against anything else that might divert from the scene in front of him. There was nowhere else he could be but right here melting under the gaze of that which branded his consequences to his brain. He was marked now. A metal plate which he could never rid himself of was nailed to his forehead. It would weigh down on his vision until his gaze could only return to his hands—those implements that had abused so. He could feel the beads of sweat drip down his back and flood his armpits as his body contorted to carry the weight of his new badge. His back hunched and his neck and shoulders folded towards one another like dishevelled cardboard and his eyes rolled back and sunk into their sockets forcing his vision to endure the sight of the plate's presence like an overhanging ridge. His elbows drew in close to his lowered chest and his fingers gnarled like rotting trees. His posterior turned to haunches and his feet to bony claws and finally the transformation was complete. Whatever he was now, he continued to look at Matt. Max was unable to speak, let alone move. Eventually Max collapsed to the ground in tears.

The rest of the night passed with speed as Max worked to remove any trace of his actions. His deformed figure dragged the body into a nearby alleyway. Later, he with his car, some washing-up liquid, sponges and a set of garden waste bags. He cocooned the body as best he could and hauled it onto the backseats and drove through the empty streets shaking at the wheel. He couldn't look in the mirror, much as he couldn't glance down any of the deserted roads he passed—both potentials were too much to contend with. What could have been a time of reflection passed with loving delicacy had become paranoia, plain and simple. Mercifully he made it out of London unmolested, and unrelenting in his decision to go West, drove deeper and deeper into the dark. With each turn not taken and each sign passed, the decision to keep going became easier and easier. Max's shattered conscience was finally quieted and its broken filigree was moved to the corners by the rise of something new. Grotesque and bulbous, a malignant growth further destroyed the elegant chandelier, tearing it down as the Kraken does unaware vessels. Shunted and pressed, the shards of this once beautiful structure were returned to their base and formless state—that of glass. Like sullied stardust cast aside this excrement drifted out of the window onto the retreating path of history decided. The streetlights turned to tracers as Max settled into himself. His rattling frame slowed first to a judder, and finally to rest under the weight of his throbbing skull.

Eventually coming round from his stupor Max turned off the main road and onto ever more winding country lanes. As the forests grew thicker it was as if he were travelling from the bronchi to the bronchioles of a smoker's lung. The rot only seemed to thicken around him, trees grew more knarred and their trunks more gnarled. They grew around his car's rear cutting off his exit and spurring him deeper. Eventually Max reached a muddy bog walking distance from the road and hopped out. He removed the body and, encasing it in further bags, lugged it towards its septic funeral. Looking down at the oily scum atop the mud he revealed the corpse. He stripped it, poured vodka over its facial cleave, and rubbed it with a rag. Then in an empty gesture of faithless resignation he donned a pair of marigolds and began to drown it. Now left with a bag of clothes and the brick he doused the latter in vodka, gave it a wipe, and returned it to his car. Driving back the way he came, Max stopped in a layby about halfway way to London, placed the brick in a pile of some of a similar colour, and dumping all the bags and clothes (including his jumper, trousers, and shoes) in a nearby barrel, burned them all with vodka and a Zippo. He stood watching the inferno and inhaling its acrid smoke, each deep breath fed the malignance in his head—and it drank greedily.

Now able to take a beat, the possession that had driven him began to fade. Yet in its throes it only demanded more; its tentacles extended out of the mirk endeavouring to pull him deeper into himself, and with each mouthful of smoke it further chanced the gaining of Max's weakening being—such things aren't cut and dry. Finally the realisation of what he'd done came to him and he fled, flapping like a ribbon in the wind. Max drove back to his flat, again in silence. He could do no more than keep his foot on the pedal and turn the wheel.

Chapter 5

Max woke the next morning to Sophie calling him. Panic of every kind folded through him to the point where he could barely hold the phone; his knuckles were clenched so hard with fear that all the superficial scabs on them burst open, plotting a map of the previous night's deeds. He sprang up and launched his phone across the room and in abject terror ran into his kitchen and took a few calming gulps from a bottle of whiskey. Naked and suckling at his bottle he looked around at the alien environment. He felt as though he was standing in a puzzle. Each step on the tiled floor was a potential choice and he, the un-weaned child, was only able to view them with downcast eyes from his bottle-bound mouth.

However, Max did eventually manage to get himself together, and mustered up the courage to check his phone.

"Good morning," Sophie had texted simply.

"Simple as that," he chuckled with exasperation! "Simple as that," he cackled! "Simple as a morning peck for a lover," he raved! His garrulous limbs were flung above him like a try for the waiting justice, whose swinging arc would mark him as a target. "A kiss! A kiss! A saving kiss," he babbled!

Yet, despite this exertion and its accompanying relief, Max was still as much the incompetent as before. The eyes of fate looked down upon him sternly, as floundering, he pathetically enwombed himself in limbo. His mania furthered and as it grew the walls began to warp pulling everything down—the air away from its occupier— eventually leaving Max alone with his desired womb realised as a liminal space, trapping him.

In interminable pain, Max began to consider what he had done; whimpering as he replayed the events of the previous evening as if it were the end of a movie. Touching his face, the still slightly swollen lumps merged to form a deformity on his left cheekbone tightly ringed by a brilliant purple bruise. As he ran his fingers around the circumference of this new feature, Max replayed gazing down at the corpse below him, and dug his nail into the skin as it went around, feeling the emotions of that look bubble up again, like lava. Matt's contributions to the night before came back to him, however,

"The assuredness with which he cut everything down to his size and arranged these figures into a mobile that rotated above his head comforting his every interaction—he was mediocrity incarnate; the face of people who didn't care because they didn't know and didn't know because they didn't care. They were incapable of either, really; they were those whose lives were lived with abounding superficiality. They were the crowd that had gathered at every execution and still did now through their phones. They were the ninety-five per cent, not bound by class, creed, colour, or gender; they were simply those who did not or could not draw what was within them, without, and inject into the world. They were those that sat, passive, and unable to shoulder their burden, and tailored the world to suit their needs, like a tailor wrapping fabric around him and fuming that he is alone in his cage."

And he, Max,

"I am the righteous fury of manifest destiny that wiped this scourge from ever particularising world I, I … I am what should be."

He was the camel who refused to have his back broken—yet this camel was well astray from deep in entropy and far from its philosophic destiny.

Now, to Max's mind, with the nettle grasped he had only to pull. And so he turned to his laptop opening various social media apps, expanding his already extensive story as *Ahriman.*

"I see now that this was what I've been needing," he said to himself, "A moment that drives me to feel what I need to feel, to become what I wish to become."

He could touch the void once again, that space outside the sun's rays, and inhabit it once more. The scaffolding he had so assiduously been constructing around it, laying it with planks and sheltering it with hanging covers, was now ready to become the support for that which would render it obsolete. On finishing his additions, he sat back smugly and admired his work.

"I will make my mark on this here world in the most appropriate way I can," he said to himself as he typed out some explanatory sentences on his profiles. They went as follows,

"I'm a general creative, singer, poet, artist …" He apologised for his "disappearance" recently, saying, "I'm so happy to be back and to reconnect with my fans after what has been an incredibly tough two years. Thank you to all those who supported me during this time, I heard every word you said! I felt that the changes I went through necessitated me removing all my work from the public eye so as to best embrace my rebirth as a person, a soul, and as a creative. My return signals my rejuvenation and a renewed desire for connection with you, my adoring fans. You can expect a rerelease of everything I've published across all platforms before, as well as remasterings of the same and signed content! For those who are unfamiliar with me and my work, I'll say this: ask my fans! I'm lucky to have a thriving community who I am in constant dialogue with—in a way my work is them! So get engaged, talk, exchange ideas, feel, and I can't wait to show you what I have in store! Ciao!"

Once done Max bought legions on legions of bots for all his accounts pumping his followers up and up, hauling in real accounts as he purchased more and more. On this first day he created *Ahriman*, as it was understood, at its height. Over the following five or six days he worked to spread himself further and to catch as much engagement as possible. In myopic focus the following month concentrated into one intense drive, with everything external winding their respective experiential threads around themselves in complete submission to the momentum.

Chapter 6

Sophie had been working exceptionally hard recently and was treating herself to a candlelit bubble bath. She had turned the lights off, lit some scented candles, spread some potpourri, and lay under the foamy mountain with a glass of wine. It was in this state that she began to reflect: she thought about work, about her life, and as she ran her fingers through the mountain of foam on her chest, her parents. She thought of her mother, and of a conversation they'd had about a week ago,

"… Sophie," she'd riposted,

"Sophie, remember you choose your problems, and as your father would say, you choose your happiness too." This had come as a response to some gripe about work, she vaguely recalled,

"How's living in London," her mother had chased eagerly,

"You must be having lots of fun,"

"I am, I am," Sophie had replied languidly. Her mind was drawn back to her painted toenails gleaming back at her over the candyfloss she'd assembled for herself and she relived the conversation.

"... Fine, fine—your father's brought me the frumpiest denim shorts I've ever seen for gardening. They're so awkward that I've considered using braces to keep them up— I'll look like an Oompa Loompa before you know it— you'll come back to a mother who bursts into song!"

"Hopefully not with the requisite spray," Sophie had thought to herself,

"But where do you go out in the evenings then, Sophie,"

"Nowhere specific," Sophie replied vaguely,

"None of the places I went to, I suppose, I imagine they've all closed," her mother giggled.

"Yes, I suppose," Sophie mumbled as she drew her wine glass left and right, growing and shrining her toes as she went.

"Sophie, you're well occupied at work and outside too, that's more than many can hope for,"

"It is ... I'm no fool,"

"Then stop behaving like one," her mother finished sharply,

"Look I need to go, but speak soon, ok."

"Ok ... In a world of hard truths Liberty, or maybe the Statue of', is queen," Sophie mused to herself.

She thought back over the last ten years. In retrospect, her teenage life was best described in the assemblage of structures that outsourced her problems to already-decided goals,

"In many ways a life of values,"

Sophie pointed out to herself, with surprise.

"Lifestyle goals, an identity, it all followed, and the fluidity, came with certain facts."

Yet were these facts realities? Were her actions, her academic choices, her degree choice and employment choices anything more than delivery systems for something more abstract? She wanted to be, and was good at, her job. Yet it was not a manifestation of what she thought she liked, but a manifestation of what she was, maybe? After all, she must have become someone underneath all of her choices, or was life merely the making of choices, and if so hadn't she done that? Whichever way she twisted the problem a tinge of something more would walk its way across her vision. Some change, so abstract that Sophie didn't know how to examine it, which she didn't have the words to unpack, made her realise just how long she had felt this pain. Yet now, for whatever reason, it was undeniable, and she felt totally unequipped to deal with it.

After Sophie had dried and dressed she wandered around her flat in a t-shirt and shorts. It was a fairly muted and minimal abode filled with sleek appliances and considered decor. Her room was across a medium-sized landing from her flatmate's and the bathroom she'd just left rotated to serve them both. Downstairs was a kitchen and dining room which abutted a large sitting room that looked out over a small garden. Most importantly, at the moment, it was near Hammersmith station and therefore convenient for her journey into South Kensington.

Sophie came to a halt in the middle of her landing and looked around the rationalised homeliness that surrounded her—it felt to be a cold embrace of her statuesque figure. She dismissed this thought and dropped downstairs to chat with Daisy whose steadying presence Sophie relished in these dead hours of increasingly regimented life.

This evening, in accordance with her name, Daisy was arranging a bouquet of flowers in a fresh vase on the dining table. She had bought them on a whim a week earlier in a bid to freshen their flat as the weather began to warm. She greeted Sophie with a silent nod as she finished spreading the firm stems around the cold glaze of their earthenware vessel. They had lived together for almost a year now and despite their ups and downs had stayed on good enough terms throughout. Theirs was an accommodating relationship; they both had enough in their lives outside the home that they weren't bound by it, which had them sometimes feeling like strangers in the other's home. Daisy worked in insurance and so had early mornings and long, sociable afternoons; whereas Sophie's journalistic sallying gave her regular hours with the occasional self-directed day. This combination of remote working and their differently timed jobs meant that they could go a week without seeing each other.

"Hiya," Daisy beamed, "How was your bath?"

"Oh lovely, so refreshing," Sophie stretched back. Salutations. These absurd formalities were not lost on each of them in their introspective moments and, having being indulged in, they returned to their respective activities: Daisy to her daisies and Sophie to a bottle of Rosé—which she suggested that they share with a cock of her head. Daisy agreed and moved her plants aside to receive the glass, eyeing Sophie playfully.

"You've got your thing tomorrow night don't you," she toyed and trailed off.

"Oh God," Sophie moaned, "Why would anyone arrange one of these things on a Monday, don't they have weekends?"

"Not some of the freaks you work with I imagine," Daisy cackled back. Sophie mock gasped to avoid replying to the barb and returned fire with,

"Well it's free booze," she winked and raised her glass to clink with Daisy's.

"Yeah but come on," Daisy pressed, "Some of those droids in HR probably spend their weekends eating cardboard."

The hilarity of this image had her squawking out the last word. Sophie took a long draught from her glass, equally bored and irritated, and letting the silence turn into a full stop, replied automatically with,

"It'll be a good opportunity for me to network. There'll be a lot of continental representation and so the prospect of wider catchment for any future exhibitions."

The statement's professional finality acted as cement laid over Daisy's chortling as much as it did a sobering reminder of Sophie's self-defined place within the world. It was, however, equivalent to dousing the conversation with liquid nitrogen, and so like on many other occasions, they were again left with each other's company. These stilted conversations were unfortunately commonplace, and though they were interspersed with frantic and gracious engagement with one another, they were the order of the day.

*

The next morning Sophie woke at eight and was on the tube after a quick shower and breakfast. It was a pity, she thought, she liked the quiet of her flat in the mornings and would have liked to wake up earlier and enjoy it for longer, but if she did the tranquillity would be broken by Daisy's disruptive presence. It felt as if she were walking the line between two realisations larger than herself. The knife's edge, on which Sophie walked between these two paradigms, was cutting deeper and baring this artificial fantasy to the world. Nothing about her life was bad. It was that simple—she knew it. Again, Sophie dismissed these thoughts and listened to some music as she made her way to South Kensington.

There, she hopped off and walked into the V&A offices—her base of operations while covering the museum's exhibition. She knew it would be a quiet day—she'd been in touch with those putting the exhibition together for months, and now that all the preparations had been made it was more a question of pulling all the strings together than of anything else. Unfortunately the morning was filled with meetings that hashed and rehashed the plans for the evening. Each member of the team had to run through their part in the affairs, outline their underpinning responsibilities, and identify their goals. Again and again the same questions were asked, the same points clarified and reclarified under the burdensome weight of bureaucratic busybodying. Detail was churned and churned until enough jargon flew around to recomplicate the issue. At this Sophie began to feel a throb deep within her as if something were crying inside of her under layers and layers of noise-dampening cloth.

Finally, lunch's breath of fresh air came, and she went with her team to a nearby cafe. Still slightly stunned they talked about their weekends, boyfriends, girlfriends, drinks, and trends. It was a pleasantly human end to a rather dry morning and on returning for the afternoon it became clear that there was little left to do. Sophie kicked back and relaxed in her cubicle, she was already dressed for the evening, so now it was simply a question of going to the museum at five to help set up and then letting the events unfold.

The afternoon wiled itself away with little interest in the bureaucratic tension of Sophie's office. Its arrested state was a breeding ground for the neuroses of the office petit bourgeois, whose molly-coddling Sophie found heart-wrenchingly dispiriting. Invisible whips seemed to crack around the office with enough frequency that they became a craven parody of a sense of community. Functionalist gristle dominated the office, making working within its walls a daily shudder through the uninspired and uninterested. However, there were a few radical eggs (good being a gift too far) who could bunch together enough failures in due diligence to pass as an original idea. The dynamism of this glitterati extended far enough to disrupt the office ecosystem, but not far enough to open a crack to the outside world. Teapot storm after teapot storm left them blind to who was drinking. Days like this had her chomping at the bit, a favourite expression of her parents, as the built-in inefficiencies were bared like proud canines, and her mind wandered back to those two, who she loved so, but felt more estranged from than ever before.

"Oh, my dear parents, how it is all beginning to fail," she uttered with choking fear.

Finally, five o'clock came and Sophie left for the exhibition space with her team. They spoke in irregular jerks due to the exasperation and excitement of the afternoon's limbo and it was only the sublimity of the pieces that brought their minds back to themselves. Their largest room had been loosely divided into a wide snaking corridor that coiled back on itself from one end of the room to the other. It was cross-cultural in its contents and a real testament to the museum's pulling power. The public was being encouraged to think broadly and to come to their own conclusions, theirs as a prompt for supposed discussions from dinner parties to op-eds. After an exhaustive, yet mercifully final, briefing Sophie and her team dispersed and she busied herself checking, just in case, that no last-minute changes had been made to the exhibition without her knowledge. This was, unlike most of their exhibitions, not made to be easily deconstructed. It was billed as a temporary exhibition, but the expectation was that it become another room in the permanent collection.

"This is something really special, you know, it's so rare to have such fundamental ... ideas ... revalued in the way they're being here, this is a building block for something totally, totally, new" The voice, her manager Jason's, finished almost rabidly as Sophie passed by the other side of the display.

By six forty-five everything had been checked and double-checked and in the final fifteen minutes Sophie and her team were treated to some champagne as their manager took the opportunity for an impromptu second final brief, a preparatory brief it seemed.

"Well done everyone," he began, "You've all done really well."

Sophie immediately switched off and watched his belly wobble as it bounced up and down on top of his belt. His gooey muffin top always intrigued her and had become a running joke with Daisy. Jason had a general plumpness to him, not fat per se: a round face, wide hips and slim calves—he was the opposite of an hourglass. His manner was questioning—he enjoyed opening debates. Sophie could imagine him opening lots of little presents at Christmas and managing to tell whoever had given it to him how essential it was before he'd even taken a look inside. It was this love of the potential that Sophie had to capture in her reporting, and her varied results tortured her. Whether or not she got what she felt was the right result, the outcome nonetheless seemed to fall flat. But, as she had unwillingly come to believe, any organisation that tended towards grand narratives fell flat because of their one-dimensionality, yet any that favoured a fractured or edgeways theme felt like a foundling in comparison to the culture of Sophie's youth.

"It was a paradox," she thought, "Projected by the short-sightedness of those above and was thus unseen and unsolvable."

By seven the drivel had abated, and Jason's foaming was replaced by champagne bubbles as he took himself off to greet the first of the entrants. The "cultural cans" began to enter through the double doors and gasped and griped in equal measure. There was a healthy dose of utter vapidity in the group, enough to curb some into an appreciative silence but not others; so began the warbling exhalations and snickering as the champagne was poured in ever more generous measures and the evening built up speed.

Jason was fast becoming the centre of attention, his rosacea led the crowd around like a set of taillights, and as the convoy grew so too did his class. In his mind he morphed from his office Mini, so fashionable and considerate, into his exhibition 4x4 (or some such lug, so esteemed) and his quickly shrinking nuance became a brush that swept all, even the art, aside in favour of strutting adjectives.

Left to their own devices Sophie and her team planted themselves around the champagne and watched the parade in front of them. How Sophie could be made to feel like one of the proletariat baffled her, but there was a clear sense amongst those who knew what they were witnessing was a shared delusion that couldn't last. This was a self-selecting party that tended towards one, and as good a compere as Jason was, he was dancing with himself.

Finally, everything wrapped up at nine and the attendees were awkwardly moved out with little grace, and all the necessary impermanences were folded and stacked away.

Jason was now pirouetting in the middle of the room, the realism of the dream seemed all to play for. It fell to Sophie, by bagsie, to end the game one way or another. She approached her inebriated superior and began passively coaxing him out to a taxi. A "Hrrumph" came in reply and to Sophie's surprise he came quietly. She awkwardly walked ahead to preserve his dignity, head semi-cocked and focused on the noises emanating from behind, leading him to the double doors. As she safely passed through, however, Sophie heard a thump as Jason fell against the wall. She quickly turned and with horror saw him weeping, head against hand, pathetically holding onto the doorframe as if it were a mast. He lurched forwards and backwards, like a mattered sail, and cooed to himself as the tears polished his reddened cheeks. Jerking his head up to meet Sophie's uncomfortable gaze he moaned,

"But it's all over Sophie, it's all over!"

Perplexed, Sophie stayed silent but Jason's pouting lips trembled,

"They're closing us down, Sophie! They're cutting the department and we won't make it!"

Now completely stumped Sophie simply returned his exclamation of their apparent decline with an extremely confused expression. Almost aghast at her lack of reaction Jason charged forward with wild eyes and flailing limbs. Suddenly very aware of Jason's thought process Sophie turned and sprinted out of the door, leaving him to fall flat on his face.

In the crisp night air Sophie jogged away and called an Uber. While waiting for it to arrive she had a pensive cigarette and considered what exactly had just happened. Whatever had or hadn't happened she had no interest in one of Jason's up-close-and-personal cultural lectures which were well-known throughout the office (as was the amount of spittle they drew) and she had no wish for one under the present circumstances. Would anything significant change? Likely not—there was the decisiveness it would require. Maybe some sort of an office culture change could occur though? This whole train of thought embarrassed her somewhat,

"What things to be thinking about…"

Chapter 7

The Uber arrived and Sophie relaxed into its plump back seat as the beauty of London unfurled on either side of her, like a tapestry. This, she thought, made everything worth it; it was for this that she did it. This city, with all its possibilities, was what drove her onward and upwards. Sophie had been raised in the countryside (Hampshire specifically) as a part of a close-knit family that prioritised efficiency above all else: her mother was very no muss no fuss and her father was bound by practicality if not by his tie. She had three brothers, all older, each of the brood was one year apart from the next, and once they'd matured beyond dolly destruction they'd all become fairly close. Sophie was often sought out as a mediator, which she enjoyed because of the inclusion despite feeling woefully unqualified—her parents fitted in, to differing degrees. That was what she'd left behind, Sophie thought to herself, as she summarised her familial ties. She had come to London to work hard and play hard and to escape the enforced fun of her hometown. There wasn't that underlying drudgery of life here in London, and the optical fun she had learned to understand was all around her. Returning to gazing at our great capital, Sophie saw the glamour of it all and drank it in in deeply until satisfied.

As they hummed through the night it began to rain. The droplets fell like coin purses exploding, sending golden glints flying all around. Soon the road was akin to something gilded, like gold leaf hammered flat long ago, and blackened with age under the streetlights The sparks overhead were beacons of structure amongst the ever-compounding ratways, they turned to tracers, guiding the city's occupants through the encroaching squalor from tributaries to rivers. At this hour the streets were clear and the progress quick,

"Long live the night," Sophie cackled to herself for this was when the city was hers; too greasy and complicated in the day. Under the night sky it was clarified under the duress of its travellers fettled to weariness. In the day the streets would choke up once again, the opulence dim under the loupe of the midday sun, as the artifice was exposed and the seething mas vied for identity, mere identity, and bubbled like an overburdened stew.

In the days Sophie's graceful and looping bounds from place to place became a tiresome hopscotch between solid ground and bog. The city her parents had traipsed around as carefree twenty-somethings had given way to an inevitable flatness necessary for morphing to fit a changing world. The apparent absurdity of this made her giggle with apprehension as she passed yet another high rise block but she knew it to be true. Money flowed more freely here than ever before, yet water flows together, and this had only widened and deepened its courses. As this natural progression occurred, floodplains, now less and less used, once waterways themselves, had become stagnant wetlands.

It was this that seemed to dry and harden every time the once exculpatory sun rose again every morning. Sophie wondered why it cleansed in the countryside and yet festered here. It seemed there was a story that had yet to be told, linking one to the other, but that moment was buried too deep within the nation's unwillingness.

On arriving home Sophie drew herself out of her berth and, thanking the driver, entered her house. She put her things down and walked into the kitchen for a glass of wine and a cigarette—luckily Daisy was in. She thought about Jason and his deterioration over the last nine months or so, the weight he'd put on, the drunkenness and the collapsing sense of self. It had been horrible to watch, and frankly, the further she went back the more she could see the increasingly toxic office politics. It was a rot from the top down she thought—hilarious for an environment that purported to work from the bottom up.

There had been yet another overhaul that began an almost weekly meeting between Jason and some part of the office about redundancies, and as these had gone on his condition had worsened. With each of these of these meetings the fat was trimmed a little, and when they had ended last month Jason was there, supposedly the steak—yet things had continued to worsen. Faced with this Sophie leant back in her chair and took a deep drag of her cigarette. As her lungs filled with numbing nicotine she saw Jason lose himself to a once well thought through job—she saw how his identity had been taken away from him little by little. What had been his fiefdom (according to her co-workers) had been broken down by his incremental demotion by those above. Now he was left with something so bureaucratised it was ungovernable, and in the invisible cage he'd been walked into he was left the keystone of an arch that stood alone, supporting nothing, unable to rise and unable to form—a prisoner of his own misunderstanding.

Concluding, the image disappeared from the wall revealing the mirror behind, presenting Sophie with nothing but herself: her lifeless expression and dulled senses stared back at her like a waxwork for a museum almost ready to open.

Disturbed by her night's thinking she had headed to bed and awakened to an empty house. She dressed and showered and headed back into the office. The rest of the week passed uneventfully. Jason returned on Tuesday afternoon and locked himself in his office for the day. Gossip buzzed between Sophie and her colleagues, but with little nectar to guzzle it died quickly. Little was said apart from a few euphemisms sprinkled in meetings. The event seemed to have been shot up a pipe to those above and wasn't to be seen again. Mission creep was developing as more and more of these issues were pulled up to the powers that be, and with that life was being removed pint by pint from the company.

This myopic obsession with what was happening around her was beginning to disturb Sophie. Friday finally arrived and she got a call from her friend Alex suggesting she come out for drinks the following evening with some of his friends. Sophie agreed and practically ran out of the office she was so desperate to leave its stagnancy behind. On arriving home she hopped straight into the bath to relax.

There she received a call from her father.

"Sophie," he began brightly, "How's your week been?"

"Boring" she replied simply. "How about yours?" she enquired excitedly, happy to hear from her father.

"Good thanks," he replied, with a hint of listlessness, "Why don't you come home Sunday morning, for the day," he stated with a slight tremble.

"Er, why," Sophie enquired.

"It would be good to see you," her father continued, "It's been a while since we've all been together and everyone's been up to so much."

"Has something happened," Sophie retorted.

"Sophie, just come home, please," her father cut in with a crestfallen tone.

"Something's happened, what's happened?" Sophie almost squawked with exasperation. Her dad replied, soothingly, "Nothing you need to worry about now, some family stuff we'll have to talk about, better sooner than later, don't worry, everything will be fine." It was at times like this, Sophie thought to herself before replying, that we really do rely on ever-soft palms.

"Fine, ok," she replied resolutely. With that the call petered out. After a couple of strained assertions from both parties, and a loving if slightly reserved sigh, Sophie hung up and let herself drop slowly into her bubbling womb.

Down she went, body pulled tight, turning to the right and lying like a foetus under the bubbles—a few seconds of warmth and succour before the bath bomb began making its way up her nose, first crackling like fireworks, but soon burning, filling her head with fire. Thrashing about, Sophie violently resurfaced sobbing, and snot rocketed into the oily water in front of her. With one giant push her sinuses were cleaned and she sat there panting and weeping slightly in the bath. She looked down at the once inviting warmth of the sustaining waters with new eyes: these were chemicals, a mixture that she was just sitting in, like a child who had never been taught to wash.

An evening of recuperation turned into a morning of recuperation and the world sat still in the unhurried heat. The afternoon sweated all across the city and people went about their business with a well-sunned timidity. Alex called again to confirm the evening's plans, no doubt some were less than willing given the heat, and Sophie assured him she'd be there. Get-togethers like the one ahead were always a chance affair she mused. People were either thrashing about in the currents of their booze-soaked teenage years, or bringing their choices to bear on those around them. This internal or external focus divided those she knew, very unequally, in favour of the former. These warriors of aggregation drove their way deeper and deeper down towards a mire of their own creation. Whatever jewels these enrichers hoped to acquire they were far less important than the rapidly constructing crown that bound them. How soon, Sophie wondered, would they bow under the weight of their affixations, and like a tree never unburdened year on year, collapse under the weight of celebrations run their course? She surmised that the world around her was one of futures seen and presents submitted, like letters, to a time capsule.

During this snatch of seasonal levity Sophie had sunk into her chair and on coming round dramatically pulled herself up. On this uncharacteristic movement, Daisy descended into their soon-to-be-sun-pit of a garden and flopped herself down next to her housemate.

"I can't," Daisy stated.

"Life," Sophie replied.

Chapter 8

As such, his entanglement with Sophie had been left to simmer and only when Max realised the flame was about to extinguish did he endeavour to save it. Sophie had been working away, feeling Max's distance from her despite the thrill of their connection, upset at what she felt was meant to be. Sophie's work had been taking her around the country a lot recently and she had enjoyed the freedom and single-mindedness it granted, particularly as it distracted her from Max. She was up in Manchester when he eventually called and she coolly answered him with the slight aloofness of one who thinks they have seen through the veil despite misunderstanding the figure underneath. Sophie told him, frankly, that she was away, and that he'd have to wait until she had returned—whenever that might be. Small talk followed, Max digested the effect of his negligence, and Sophie walked out to her room's balcony for a cigarette. Previous relationships came to mind, each returned to her now as anxieties of the time. Retrospection seemed to reveal the nub of each, yet not their larger meaning. If each was merely what she had needed at the time, and each had built her up to be the person she was to be, who was she now? She certainly wasn't the sum of her relationships, yet she had poured herself into each and only taken back what was useful. Yet, she had no idea who she was. It was as if her attachments were ancillary to everything she was now, yet a central part of who she had become. Sophie couldn't extricate herself from her decisions, she couldn't find herself without what she felt herself to be, so what was she? Rolling around her head, moving in and out of her cares, the question came and went as she finished her cigarette and settled herself into the room.

After unpacking Sophie decided to have a wander around and find somewhere for dinner. She weaved her way through the city's post-industrial refurb finally settling on a hole-in-the-wall under a railway arch. The waiter, about her age, bounced up to her and offered her a menu and after running through the specials left her mercifully quickly. Alone, Sophie's eyes drifted around the room sliding from face to face as she got a sense of what sort of people came to this neon-lit place. Her fellow diners were almost all of that early-twenties to mid-thirties glossy faced type—anodyne drifters. They were all, sadly, defined by the economic malaise that they were so tightly caught in; unable to put down any meaningful roots, thus taking their pleasures conventionally in exciting, pre-packaged fun. Those at the upper end of the catchment had been failed by those who were there to represent them; their right-footed rise to nothing had left them worse off than their parents. At the lower end expectations were defined by what they saw happening to those older than them; seeing them begin to bow under the ever-more tangible weight of stagnation. Yet as the possibility of creating something of their own slipped away, the reality of what was already theirs, that which they'd inherited, was degenerating at the front of their minds—and so restaurants like these were created. Theirs was a world in which entertainment was becoming reality in the worst way possible—and yet it was so clearly unavoidable. Intractability defined all they saw and thus, little by little, their experience of life was changing from that of previous generations. History no longer seemed to repeat itself, instead, incidentals changed, and they, the people, obediently changed with them. As dynamism left the world it found its new home in the tumultuous realm of each individual's psyche—perfect continuation.

Sophie finished and paid for her colourful and somewhat satiating meal. Deciding that she might as well face a bar she continued to explore her surroundings until she came to another squeaky-clean den of debauchery. Inside, Sophie was confronted by a parade of the considered, and as was common these days, she yielded to its "niceness." That was the problem, Sophie mused as she sipped a glass of wine, "I'm sleeping walking through an over-considering world." It wasn't that she wasn't thinking of others, she sighed and tutted to herself, although she was grown up enough to admit she liked a man who thought of her a little less than she did. It was just simply so fashionable to think of others that she wondered who, if anyone, would be able to move it all forward.

"Everyone knows you've got to do things for yourself," she surmised,

It felt like the coup de grace of platitudes rather than a conceptual preface to be walked away from. But it was better than saying whatever the right thing was.

"And that's what I've been doing", yet it was beginning to dawn on her that this truism was more an indication of raft hopping than of path forming. As Sophie looked back at her short life she saw a succession of currents that she had navigated and which had brought her, like a dignitary on a pleasure cruise, to dock at the bottom of an escalator. What about her friends and their choices? They had been given the same options and they had all chosen what they knew.

Finally Sophie waved off her introspective cowl and, looking around this new establishment, caught eyes with one of a few lads at the bar who nodded back at her. Pretending not to notice, Sophie continued to turn her head past him and landed on a few, gender-differentiated, groups of people about her age. Thumbing through them as though they were a filing cabinet she pulled out the most interesting to look at: a striking face with stark eyebrows and full lips,

"A little like Max," she thought, "Whose tightly curled hair wavered with each bob and weave of his chatty head."

Sophie sipped her drink and turning back came face to face with the man at the bar. He had walked over and was in the process of sitting next to her. Jumping a little inside she greeted him with a reserved, if a little mocking,

"Hello." Sitting askance, he twisted his body towards her,

"Hey, I saw you looking at me." His sluggish eyes and expectant gait spoke of a long day in the pub, and his smelling like a brewery confirmed it.

"Hi," Sophie grimaced back. Her face shallowed into a well-practised and unilateral mask of

"Leave."

Luckily for her, however, his drunkenness got the better of him. As he was twisting around further he knocked his pint all over the table and, in a truly pathetic fashion, managed to fall off his chair in shock. Sophie jumped up to save her belongings, holding her drink as she looked down at the would be flirt. She pitied him, herself, and the whole fucking world.

*

Back in London Max was beginning to miss Sophie and his thoughts of her grew and grew until they filled every hour he was away from his laptop. Yet as his work consumed him these hours grew fewer. His pining was gradually pressed harder and harder into the walls of his mind until it became a shattered mirror in the corner of a long-forgotten attic. He was building his house, he thought, on foundations of himself and as it grew so too did that which underpinned it, until he had the whole mansion to himself. He was a lucky man he thought, a truly lucky man.

As his digital presence grew, Max's mental state declined. His efforts moved him into people's lives and in this, the fourth dimension, he grew outside of his own actions. As Max became more successful his virality increased and his myth was burnished by each supercilious article. All the while, however, the intricacies of his creative development were being clarified and lacquered; layers of varnish applied by an army of loyal followers. Those who saw ever deeper into his work and life became, like a pack of hungry dogs, vitriolic in their interactions with one another as their reverence of "*Ahriman*" turned him into an interpretable foundation myth. Day by day the line he had drawn between his early circumstances and his current success was being separated into disparate strands.

Max was no longer the captain of his soul. He was in fact becoming more craven by the day, and as his deformed figure settled it drove deeper into its surroundings. Forced to work longer and longer hours, visions of Matt's corpse visited him ever more frequently and their intensity grew as their complexity decreased. What had begun as horrifying walk-throughs became distillations of that accursed evening. His mind was working to move past it, like secateurs cutting through a great gorse, but it still left jagged remains that cut him dear. These lesions yawned and their bile spewing mouths could only be numbered when clad in the cold. The images paraded before his waking eyes like display cases frozen in time as he propelled himself faster and faster.

Despite his terror Max fell into each one, reliving the night with that version of himself at the helm. The self-righteous fury that bubbled up with each viewing provided a respite from his pain even as it warped his mind into shifting blame onto anything other than his lethal arc. First he blamed Matt, the provoker, the epitome of everything wrong with the world. Secondly he blamed society for coddling men like Matt into abominable self-satisfaction while those like him had to fight for their codification. They bettered the system by breaking it and re-building it—they were propagators. Finally, he blamed that which had always hung around him like damp—ill luck and damnation. This final one bled thickly like a dredged-up artery, and as Max held it phallically, his jaded internal spewed out as a fountain of possible experiential balm.

The inner child, the cooing calmer, gave back all that was dumped on him. It was infinite and could bear the burden of unrealised need and wasted desire. It was potential incarnate and thus the perfect receptacle for all incapable souls struggling under the yoke of their own inability.

In his brief moments of exhausted respite he sent off a few texts to Sophie. Their romance was not quite extinguished. His odd blow of the embers, along with their mutual appreciation of one another, kept the spark from retreating into the past. Yet as Max looked at himself in the mirror of his locked screen, what he saw was further and further from his recollection of himself. As he waited for each of Sophie's tepid replies, he noticed how his once angular and striking face had softened and mellowed like butter. Where there had once been directing vertices there were now smoothed, pallid surfaces, mottled with discolourations like the marbling of a rainbow. His eyes had risen to the surface like the oily backs of two breaking blue whales, and under this his nose had buttoned and his lips had drawn. He resembled an E-fit more than anything else.

His once definite face had become one of many and a truly forgettable one than that.

Max worried about how Sophie would see him now. He wasn't what she had met not by any means. He was depleted in ways he couldn't articulate. It was as though drips had been inserted all over his body, on parts he couldn't even name, draining him day by day. His self-loathing skyrocketed as the situation dawned on him. The horrors of his actions reproduced even more quickly, and he was wrapped further and further up in himself.

Sophie was now back in London and allowing herself a little hope. She paid more attention to his replies as she sipped her morning coffee on the way to work. She knew he worked at odd times and so didn't think too much of the late texts. They weren't lewd enough to be booty calls, but their content troubled her. What had started vivaciously had turned morose, and from there it felt like being pawed by a dying cat. Her faith came in ebbs and flows and at each plateau the content was further exposed, leaving her more confused than before.

Of course her life had moved on—not that Max seemed aware of this. She'd met others, work was going from strength to strength, and her friends were as loyal as before. She began to think about the future and what it meant to her.

Something was being built, but Sophie didn't identify it as hers and this niggling feeling of purposeless sent her into herself. Sophie did not relish the experience. Introspection brought her back to the reactionary within—so too did the glossed artifice of plastic smiles and apathy. Hers was definitely a journey for there was no place that could hold all she was. But was it á la Mary Poppins, bicycling through the sky—merely a spoonful of sugar? Burdened by this uncomfortability she was more pensive than usual.

It was in this state of outward calm that she ran into Alex one afternoon and heard the news of Matt's disappearance. The gap between his death and widespread knowledge of it could apparently be explained by his frequent travelling for work and his frosty relationship with his close family. Therefore, by the time a missing person's report was identified as the next step and Matt's headshot was seen across social media, the memory of that night in the pub had left her mind almost entirely—apart from meeting Max, of course.

"Have you heard what happened," Alex had asked when they ran into one another,

"No."

Alex had explained the situation, and so began their awkward recollection of Matt's difficult character. He had been abrasive, they agreed—that was the end of that, they agreed. Promising to notify one another if they heard anything, they parted ways with a little of each of their respective reservations left hanging in the air. Sophie thought about Matt, how she hadn't really liked him, how it seemed few did, and she wondered what would come of the investigation. She bit her lip, bobbing her head back and forth a little as she realised the obvious: if she were expected to do as much Alex had just asked, Matt's family could not be doing much. The whole situation saddened her.

Matt definitely wasn't a bad man, Sophie assured herself desperately, just uncharismatic, and he had paid for that dearly.

"He must have led a lonely life," Sophie thought, "Defined by his desires no doubt."

He'd struck her as a man who based his worth on his decisions. But they bookended him. These visions of his desires had rendered him trapped within a cage that he couldn't know the bars of.

Sophie was not a little embarrassed when her mind slipped to her own situation, and she wondered what the world would hold for her if she continued to follow her path. In sight of this potential, Sophie quickly dashed the thought and forced her focus back to Matt and his unfortunate disappearance. There was very little information about what might have happened. The Police had said he could have gone missing anytime from the night at the pub to a week later.

It was all very vague.

Together they decided that the best course of action was to spread the word as much as possible and wait for the Police to catch up. Who knew what they'd actually manage to do? Looking around at the cold, grey world Sophie felt like an urban cowboy, trotting her path through the arid desert of falsehood.

*

Max, on the other hand, was drowning in his own. Surrounded by mirrors of his own lies he finally stepped outside after a month and hobbled down the street. His bank account was dried up from food orders and his sun-starved, emaciated body was draped with clothes which had once fit. The rays were dizzying and, blinded, he had to steady himself like a drunk. As he shuffled towards Tesco to pick up something to cook, Max began to grow sick with fear as he caught the stares and glances of his fellow walkers. Disturbed, his inner began to bubble and burn with unspeakable fury at all the mediocrity that surrounded him.

"Bots, NPCs," they were—"Empty headed mannequins being moved by whatever once created momentum."

Growling, spitting, and wiping his mouth on his sleeve, sweat formed a layer between his skin and clothes. The sun, the clarifier, only aided in the degeneration of his mutated form. Max couldn't hide from it—he was tortured by it and forcing himself to move faster and faster, he took sanctuary in the safety of the cold disinfected air of a supermarket.

Once home, and with the help of some whiskey, Max straightened himself out with some hygiene and resolved to cook a decent supper. To his surprise his efforts were rewarded with a call from Alex, whose explanation of the events regarding Matt almost had Max keeled over and vomiting into the bin. Croaking back an acknowledgement and grunting some assurance that he'd do what he could, Max hung up the phone and screamed as long and as loudly as he could. Visions of that night charged towards him like a deer to headlights and he could do nothing but stay where he was. He watched himself over and over again and with each replay his shining chest heaved and bile dribbled onto the wooded kitchen floor.

After a while his nose began to burn red and his raw flaking lips dried. Finally Max crouched down and began to cry. Thick salty tears filled his palms, and a shade appeared in the dancing glass that formed. This amorphous entity swayed like a genie, confident in its newfound freedom outside the lamp. A vaporous substance seemed to steam out of his hands, and what followed was a coronation of his suffering—a deep, thundering laugh. It grew and reverberated like sonar plotting the room around a prostrate Max. All around him the walls shuddered and the air fizzed, splitting into grainy colours. Out of his hands emerged, limb by limb, a chimaera made of onyx. Clad in the smoke emanating from its nose, it gripped Max's skull, pulling itself up to his pale face and setting its eyes in front of his.

The being's fingers hooked around Max's lips and drew his mouth and eyes back into a maniacal grin. After seductively nibbling at the back of his neck it came to his left ear,

"Hello Max," it whispered, letting out a sulphurous breath which set Max's teeth chattering, "What a pleasure it is for us to finally meet."

Max remained mute as the chimaera continued,

"What you've done Max can never be undone you see. And I'm the result. I'm the weight you'll have to bear for the rest of your life—for sins like this haunt you until the day you die…"

"Well, if you're to be there forever, what should I call you?" Max stammered back. The chimaera giggled his reply,

"Ever the supplicant, ye spineless idolator! I am *Ahriman* and you are mine!"

"What do you want with me then?" Max replied desperately, "Punishment?". *Ahriman* laughed even louder now,

"Oh, were it that simply, my darling maquette. You are mine to torture, yes, but you are also mine to be served. You, the self-declared arbiter, have now been arbitrated, and have been declared a horse to my chariot—just as you carry me now."

Max began to sob under the weight of this apotheosis and his prostrate figure addressed the mirror in front of him. His eyes were averted from the rider on his neck.

"Please no—I regret everything. I'll do anything to rectify my actions, anything, I beg you! I throw myself at your master's feet and beg forgiveness."

Ahriman's laugh grew into a roar as he replied, "You fool, he isn't my master and you've simply been judged by your own standards. You'd be attempting to convince yourself, but that opportunity passed long ago."

Perplexed, Max replied, "So there is no court I could be brought to as a shackled prisoner, no judgement to appeal?"

"No, you fool," *Ahriman* growled, "You are the author of your destruction and if you don't understand that then maybe you will in time."

Now completely lost, Max looked at the crumbs on the carpet and then promptly vomited.

*

All the while, however, Max's digital presence was growing, and it was demanding more and more attention. The trappings of fame were coming his way, and urgent appeals were being made for his appearance at various events in the upcoming summer. What had in itself been a nervous push had now devolved into a flurry of different directions, each one assured by their set of devout enablers. Fast becoming a movement, it picked up more and more oppositional self-definers, and as its message diversified, its thrust strengthened and unified. *Ahriman* was fast becoming an emotional shorthand for anti-establishmentarianism—it was a broad church label applicable to failed social interactions as much as to institutional failures. Its followers busied themselves furthering the flourishing project for their absent King. The omnipotence began to become palpable. The endorsements became cultural.

*

Later that evening Anna called and disturbed Max's nightmare.

"Why don't you come over," she said, "I'm on my way back from the office and ordering something, what do you want? It'll be here when you arrive."

In blind confusion, Max agreed. He cleaned himself vigorously and dressed hoping that he could erode the pain that had overcome him. Unfortunately, however, all his efforts yielded him was a slight sheen on his translucent skin and some entertainment for the gleeful *Ahriman*. The chimera would coil and climb around his body, always an inch away from Max's pawing hand, and cause him to jerk and fall against the glass—an absentmindedly manipulated puppet.

On arriving, Max smoothed back his hair, knocked on the door, and listened to the sound of Anna coming to him.

"Hello," she purred, "Why don't you come inside."

She had ordered them some pizza and as she led him into the kitchen her retreating hips betrayed a giddying joy. She had abandoned her characteristically punctilious gait and this unusual step was tinged with a slight vivaciousness at the expense of her normal officiousness. Beckoning him into the kitchen with a painted nail, still quixotic, she bade him sit on the nearest stool as she furled herself on top of the opposite one.

"So," pressing her hands down her thighs, "Things have changed."

Ahriman played with a letter to the right of Anna's glass of wine and ran his grotesque nostrils over its window. Max glanced at his tormentor and back to Anna, listening as she explained:

"I'm moving Max, you see, and so we aren't going to be able to see each other like we used to, in fact likely ever again. I wasn't planning to end it, I just don't know when we'll see each other again, and I thought you should know, and that's really it."

The desired impact of this statement was no doubt lessened slightly due to the proclamation of damnation Max had received earlier,

"What?"

"It's as I say Max," she replied curtly. "We cannot see each other anymore due to my moving abroad, unforeseen circumstances, I'm simply explaining that to you." Max's head throbbed,

"So, what the fuck am I doing here then?"

Anna joyfully let his abruptness run over her like a gratifying breeze,

"Well, I thought it was only fair we did this in person as we've been doing this a long time, what do you think?"

Still blank, Max replied, "Alright, thanks, where are you going?" Anna fluttered her eyelashes up to the heavens and reached for the letter,

"Well," she began, "I've been invited to Monaco, and I think I'll be staying there! I'm getting out of my lease here," she continued, "And I'm moving within a month or two. And I won't have time to see you."

It was on this that they parted.

*

Later Max realised he hadn't asked Anna what she was doing in Monaco or who'd invited her, but as he thought back on the last few years he realised he didn't care—

"In either case, she clearly doesn't want me to know."

What had worked about them, he was reminded, was that they'd both known the niches in each other's lives and it was into them that they had fitted perfectly. It was so perfectly artificial that both could honestly walk away from it without any lingering emotions. In fact, it was like turning the light off on leaving a room, but instead of walking away down the hall, the room simply disappears behind you and you're left with all the options you wanted anyway.

"It was a credit to their degradation of themselves," he pondered; "We've managed to spend so much time together without growing together, or even sharing anything beyond the obvious."

Max moved on from Anna and back to *Ahriman*, whose who's horrid fondling hadn't ceased all evening.

"Why did you wave that letter at me," he asked sharply,"

"We all need to know the consequences of our actions, don't we" the chimera laughed back.

Not wanting to explore what this meant, Max kept his mouth shut tightly and eyed the pavement warily as he hurried back to his flat.

On arriving Max was greeted by a noise—a tap, tap, tap—the creator of which he couldn't see. He stopped and looked at his door and the taps grew into thunks. Max began to sweat and he could feel it being rubbed into the small of his back by *Ahriman*'s muscular tail. The chimaera began to laugh a slow deep rumble, but this grew into shuddering howls. Then, just as this cacophony crescendoed, a figure began to appear in front of the door. At first it was a shimmering outline, but after filling out it became a silhouette. Finally colour inked its way into the body like blood through arteries, and Matt's swaying figure was revealed to Max.

The spirit swung around and, regarding Max with its good eye, lurched towards him as blood poured from its face, soaking its clothes and flying everywhere with each step. It grabbed Max by the head and pressed its waterfall of a face to his, forcing the bleeding into Max's mouth and choking him. The chimaera, meanwhile, wrapped his tail around their necks, holding them together, covering them with sooty marks as he forced his lurid snout into any available gap between them, breathing sulphurous fumes into their faces. Max was choking. Bending lower to catch his breath, but so too did Matt—their bodies formed a bridge and they swallowed one another—only further as they went.

On the floor, Max looked at an enormous pool of blood left by Matt's charging, yet his attacker had disappeared. Scrambling around wretchedly, Max felt a lump form in his stomach. It grew denser and more defined. He could feel its smooth surface and spherical shape and the four prongs that grew out of it. The onyx object had taken shape, and *Ahriman*'s howls became a revolting cackle that trailed off with each beat of Max's deadening heart. On his hands and knees, Max looked down as the blood evaporated and the chimera grew, further covering his back and digging its claws into his shoulders and hips. It seemed to be digging a hole downwards into his upper back. At this realisation, Max went out cold.

Chapter 9

Max awoke to the nudging and murmurs of a voice guiding him out of Hades. Little by little it drew him back into the land of the living, picking off each putrid tentacle as it went. Finally, on turning over, he opened his eyes to Sophie's welcoming smile.

It retreated immediately, however, and gave way to the blank and far less welcoming face of Alex who simply asked,

"Didn't manage to make it home, mate?"

Max, now on his back, looked at the pair as a crab does its captors and mumbled a lost retort.

"We need to talk, mate," said Alex, "This thing with Matt is still going." As he struggled up Max heard a faint giggle but paid it no attention,

"Oh yeah?"

"Yeah," Alex replied, "Is there somewhere we can grab a coffee?"

On finding a greasy spoon, they ordered Full Englishes and Sophie ordered scrambled eggs. Once they'd received their food and Alex and Sophie had finished with their furtive glances and longing looks, the latter went to the loo and Alex began:

"Look mate," he explained, "Matt's still missing, and the Police have the view that something's happened to him. They're digging into his family at the moment and they're going to start digging into us soon—and everyone at the pub the other night. There isn't much to be done beyond wait, but just in case you've anything untoward knocking about, you know the sort of thing I mean—they *will* be coming to your flat." Max stared back vacantly, but eventually replied, "Yeah cheers mate" and, giving a few nods, awkwardly went back to his food.

Alex's advice fell on deaf ears as Max's head swam in the brackish water of sorrow and desire. Sophie returned—next to him sat someone the likes of which he'd never met before. This was love, he was sure of it—yet all around him was the stench of his, so unequivocal, indignity. She was just about visible out of the corner of his right eye. She was a lighthouse, able to guide him to whatever lay past his current condition. A part of him felt compelled to throw himself at her feet and to worship her transformational power. He wanted Sophie to raise him up, to inspire the strength necessary to overcome his turpitude, and to clad him in the armour of purpose and aspiration. However, edging his head around towards her, Max saw not the enveloping and womblike embrace of a potentially coddling and fictitious saviour, but the listless face of a woman uninspired at her love's depletion. This vacancy lent Sophie an impassiveness that further coloured their dynamic with heroic splendour in the eyes of that latent flash of childhood.

Alex, irritated at his friends' mellowness, pressed on and started running through possible scenarios of Matt's disappearance, becoming more rattled with every utterance:

"… and lastly, I suppose, is murder," he trailed off. The horror of the statement settled in the middle of the conversation, all were silenced and left alone by its all consuming presence.

*

The triplet disbanded soon afterwards, and each went their separate ways. Both Max and Sophie wanted the other to say something, but neither was able to bridge the gulf of their newfound isolation. What for Sophie was the verbalisation of a fear that had become harder and harder to ignore, was exactly what Max had known since he'd birthed *Ahriman* from his cupped hands—drawing it from the net into the real world. With this acceptance he walked back to his flat—the point in his back where the chimaera had dug was burning and the inflammation was making its way towards his guts. Max's vainglorious discovery of love had him imagine the peerless figure of Sophie as he walked, but as each detail sharpened she withdrew from his vision, as if viewed backwards through an extending lens. were hurtling away from one another and towards being worlds apart.

Soon each would have their own problems and more importantly each their own solutions and that double helix of love, which could bear each safely through the unknown, would fall apart like a chandelier to the revolution.

Yet all this pontificating disgusted Max and his anger boiled away these idyllic narratives,

"I'm a murderer. I've killed someone. And retreating into soul-soothing myths doesn't change this fact. Nor do they possess any useful truth, they belong to a world completely removed from this. I am what I am and despite the overwhelming nature of my crimes, I must confront them. I can't owe it to myself," he continued, "I'm too disgusted, but I can owe it to those who think something of me"—on that Sophie's graceful step turned into the corner of his mind.

Max couldn't return to the burial site, he knew that, it would risk inditement – and yet he had to face himself.

"I must understand the extent of what I've done ...," he reasoned, and yet on this, *Ahriman* flipped around in front of him and forced himself into Max's face. Max screamed in pain and saw all that had occurred that night in lurid detail right before his eyes,

"But yet my child you can see all you are with only a brief thought—there is no need to return," *Ahriman* boomed.

Max dug his fingers between his and *Ahriman*'s flesh and bellowed back,

"Because I will not be your plaything, you revolting devil! Cast yourself away and let me face myself without your rancid tinging you bellicose bastard"!

"But I am no aggressor," *Ahriman* seductively replied.

I am a soother." Its tail smoothed Max's jacket,

"I am the oil that curries favour from your crabbing gears. You can't go on without me and you don't want to be able to. What lifeblood you imagine you have is a falsity you reinforce with your pathetic tales—but now you have me. I will sustain you. Just look at what you have done with your career, your dishonesty and degeneracy sustains it and look how well it does. There are legions of peons that glorify and flagellate themselves at altars to you, thinking they are arbiters of change. Their lifecycle of devotion and revulsion takes place in a glass jar that is but one of the thriving populations of your sitting room's shelves. From your table you can view your trapped Tinkerbells like the playthings they are and shake them up like snow globes at your leisure. You are the collector and you have forged each grain of sand into a glass cage for your serfs. In doing so you have solidified the dessert—and you cry for change. You fool, you are the change man has been cravenly dreaming of its whole existence and you must press on!"

Max staggered back as the tirade finally abated and, appalled, tore the chimaera off his face and charged home. Yet the thing danced and pranced on his shoulders as he ran, and once he'd slammed the door behind him it was as present as it had been before.

*

Later, and a little calmer, he called up a couple of his poker friends and after a brief explanatory apology for his dropping off the radar suggested a game that weekend—which he would organise. Four yesses returned and he phoned the Dog and Duck, booked the room, and relapsed into a gliding repose through the seated journey of his imagination. He was being borne along a river in a punt with a flat floodplain on either side. There, at regular intervals, were scenes from his life that could each, he was sure, be stepped into as an invisible observer. Yet he was unable to move or turn around to ask the helm to land the vessel. As this realisation dawned the sky folded in on itself become a shallow tunnel that blacked out his journey. Each of the scenes turned luminescent, and what had been a landscape of dancing nymphs became an ever more complicated kaleidoscope of merging visions which crowded their unwitting victim. This paralysing display disturbed Max so much that he was able to rip himself around and regard his mute guide. He was shocked to discover that a haggard version of himself, drawn with sewn-up lips, stared back vacantly.

Max launched awake and threw himself off the armchair and onto the floor. A hairy claw raised his head,

"Where did you go," it suspiciously asked,

Ahriman's nails dug into Max's sharp chin, puckering his yellowing skin.

"What," Max replied dumbly.

"You heard me you fucking imp," the beast retorted, dropping its high tones of submission. Ahriman hit Max and, continued, "Where did you fucking go?"

*

After he'd washed and dressed, Max left his flat and wandered around a nearby park. Families played, friends laughed, and a buoying glow reminded him of a time long ago. In that lifetime there were no devils, no sickness, and the past and future fell away from him. Now gliding along, as those around him gave way, he returned the favour and so began a dance of gestures and nodded acknowledgements. This Elysian frolic gifted individuals roles, dignifying subconsciously yearned for dynamics and yet they weren't caricatures—they were the roots of their individuality, they were the pots that formed the soil that grew the flower. His previous lens, it now seemed, had forced the world into monochrome.

Chapter 10

After this episode Max found himself on the river walking along towards the city. His glow preceded him and on realising he had plenty of time before his appointment at the Dog and Duck he decided to stop for a quick one. To his surprise Anna was inside. She sat at the bar shifting her gaze between her phone and a glass of wine. She was equally surprised to see Max and when he sat down beside her, she asked sharply, "What are you doing here?"

"I could say the same to you," Max replied, disguising his confusion with the scrape of the bar stool, "Bit lowkey for you," he continued.

Anna replied, with her eyes downcast, "Yes, I was rather hoping to avoid anyone I'd know."

This admission literally floored Max: the combination of sitting down absent-mindedly and jerking aghast, caused him to fall off his chair. They gazed at one another, one on the floor and one seated. The absurdity of the situation was somehow lost on Anna as shame seemed to blind her. However, the other patrons were not so hoodwinked and they roared with laughter.

"Honestly everything's just so totally fucked," she continued with her eyes still downcast towards the floor where Max had only just returned from.

"What," Max moaned, grasping his pint and nodding at the barman's giggling grin.

"I'm just so ashamed, I feel so stupid," she drove on gesticulating and wide-eyed.

"Well, why," Max said impatiently as he rubbed his head.

"The job's a joke," she squeaked, "It's a fucking joke and I've jumped in head fucking first!" She slapped the table. "The man wants me as his PA or whatever and as far as he's concerned I'm some escort who'd catch the drool out his mouth in mine if I could—he's a fucking pig," she yelled!

"Oh," Max replied, confused, "Oh well I'm sorry—a bit of a cunt by the sounds of things."

"Ha" she snorted, "But I've given up everything for it," she continued.

"Well… surely it's not the end of the world, shit happens, you can move on."

"No, you fucking moron," she exploded, "I've humiliated myself. I bet everything on this and it's all fallen through and now I'm utterly adrift. I gave everyone the old fuck and duck and now I'm to crawl back to their cackling maws begging forgiveness."

"Right, I see your problem now," Max laughed back.

"Shut up," she replied sharply as she landed a maternal slap on his upper arm, "You're a terror."

Max picked up on the tonal change and could feel the request bearing down on him, its drawn-out obviousness was antithetical to the giddiness he had felt once upon a time. Anna snaked her arm under, around, and on top of his and delved her fingers in between his.

"You should have a dinner party you know," she purred, "I'll do all the cooking etc for you, you choose the guests, and we host it at yours."

"God you're unbelievable aren't you," Max replied, sighing, as he turned away to gaze at the TV screen.

"Oh, come on, think of everything I've done for you over the years," she retorted with exasperation, "Amelia, Rachel, all that bollocks with Ben—you've got to help me out."

"Aren't you the co-conspirator now, dear lover," Max snorted.

"Yes" she replied curtly, satisfied by his understanding. "We're good together and you know it, we've always been there for one another in a very practical way." As she laid out their history her fingers slapped the table in a rhythmic tempo, "everyone's stepped off and on the stage at one time or another except us, because we hold things together. We have consistency and precedent when everywhere around us lacks it—there's value here." She squeezed his hand as she finished her speech. Max giggled to himself as she wrapped up her campaign.

"Look Anna, I've got to go. Good luck with everything, but I really can't help you." As he raised himself off the stool Anna grabbed him and hissed,

"Fuck you, you fucking cunt," and shoved him backwards. Max caught himself and, wheeling around, sped out of the door.

*

As he turned onto the footpath and continued down the river, Max walked his mind through all the events Anna had brought up. They seemed immaterial in retrospect, he thought to himself, but had needed real attention at the time.

All were social snafus or actual social fucking catastrophes that their friends barely mentioned because of how awkward they had been. Anna was right; people had come and gone and 'the group' had gradually shrunk, paring itself down. Yet that process of ostracisation and alienation hadn't been some great epic, had it? It had really been a process of group chats changing sizes and big parties with changing guest lists—it was hardly Shakespearean. Anything that he and Anna had created together had been a dam, insulation against the rest of the world.

With that the ephemerality of the last five, seven, nine, years began to reveal itself like junk under a retreating tide. A long sunny afternoon paddling in the shallows with a foot touching the remnants of past dramas, had become a walk through a cemetery of the discarded. Each toe that snagged a corner further embellished the undersea unknown and caused pleasantly sanitised ripples for the rest of them. Those who he and his friends had assumed were watching from the shore with yearning eyes and from the safety of solid predictability must have laughed at all the filth they found themselves in. If this picturesque sea view had ever existed outside of their narcissism, it certainly didn't exist anymore.

"Anna must know that on some level," he decided, "Else she wouldn't have asked me to host the dinner party." Her needing something from me is antithetical to what kept the house of cards constructed all around us. We were above needs, above mere humanity, and victim to that which we chose to allow our attachment to—which was nothing. We played with ourselves and we played with each other. We were ultimately static and a joke to those living their lives around us. "Others will dig back into that fantasy, surely," he continued, "Others need it too and they're certainly not ready for reality. But then again," he countered, "I'm the one thinking about this, taking a miserable walk down the river."

He was the one decrying that which he was hung up on. After all, whether you're tying or untying the hangman's noose—it's still your rope.

This unnerving realisation stopped him in his tracks and had him gazing down at his hands. He had used them to extinguish Matt and now he was using them to construct a cage around himself stocked with implements for flaying, stabbing, and crushing. His physical form, it seemed, was as morphable as his online persona. Yet where was the pain when his digital profile was ruptured and torn by his devout acolytes, inanimate in their prostration and damaging in their purpose? What was drawn by their lacerating actions? What did he lose with each impassioned exertion? This problem weighed heavily on his mind as his placid face turned into a warring grimace. Max was at the end of a long rope, tied tighter and tighter around him, dragging him forward—stumbling like a slave to be devoured before the whooping Coliseum crowds. The heat of the sun beat down and he could hear the bloodlust, but where were the lions that would finally do for him? Where were those singular in purpose, righteous in desire, and brutal in execution? Where were the claimants to his soul before the destruction of his once dignified human form?

Chapter 11

The journey home was as uneventful as she'd expected, and Sophie shot through the countryside watching the once wild land, now bound by plant and plough, present itself to her.

"These patterns," she thought wistfully to herself ... She loved that she could walk through them and that she could play like a child in these remains of a more connected time.

The houses turned to cottages and the tiles to thatch, and with each detail Sophie lost herself a little more to the land around her. Her youngest brother, Arthur, met her at the station in the battered family Golf. He was short, stocky and red, like a pint of ale with the light shining through, and when he saw Sophie he scooped her up, practically throwing her over himself in his excitement. The pair had always been close but with Arthur now committed to farming they saw less of each other than ever.

"How are you," he asked excitedly as they strolled back to their green buggy.

"Happy to be home, frankly, I need a break from London ..." Sophie pulled herself back—she had been about to lose herself in an explanation of all that had happened since they'd last seen each other,

"What's happened to Mum?" Arthur's face dropped and let out a long exhale,

"I was hoping I could distract you a little longer," he mumbled dejectedly. "Look it's best we do this at home, it's a difficult one." Sophie was surprised by the mollification this statement caused,

"No doubt as to why they sent Arthur," she mumbled to herself.

They got into the car and set off in silence. Sophie did her best to put whatever was coming out of her mind and tried to enjoy the scenery. Unfortunately she had to appreciate her limitations in this task, and as the sun continued to boil the car's black interior, her thoughts turned towards what lay ahead. It was obviously a family emergency but unless it was a dramatic accident she had no idea what it was. She was sure her father wouldn't have been able to hide his pain over the phone. He must have known about it in advance, yet why wasn't she aware of it? She hadn't been away long enough for something to develop in her absence, so had it been around longer than that? Was it predictable? Was that why her father had been so flat in tone over the phone?

All these thoughts swam through her as she sat, parched, inside the little box, cognisant of only the sweat she couldn't shake off.

*

The pair arrived home without having said a word to one another, they were deep down within themselves. A silent walk up to the house followed, and there was a long pause before the door opened. Here, Arthur looked at Sophie. He squeezed her upper arm and kissed her on the head. His looking down at her with those morose eyes brought some despair, once buried deep, up to visit upon her. They entered and were greeted by the rest of the boys standing awkwardly around the kitchen. The two oldest, Edward and Jonathan, were leaning on opposite walls facing one another. Their father, Alastair, was standing at the head of the table with his arms outstretched leaning on the back of his chair. Faced with this picture Sophie felt a fury rising within her. In keeping with the rest of the family Arthur finally positioned himself two thirds of the way down the mahogany table between Sophie and their other siblings.

Sophie looked from one to the other with growing expectation and decreasing patience.

"What is it then," she blurted out awkwardly.

"Let's sit down," her father uttered calmly, gesturing to the table.

"Fine," Sophie replied sharply, "What is all this, where's mum?" With that, all the boys' eyes sank.

"Please, let's just sit," Her father spoke weakly as if a wounding spear had finally been removed and some aged blood spilt from its residence.

"So, it's about mum then—what is it?," Sophie shrugged and stepped towards the table, one step closer to tying this up, she thought to herself,

"Yes, it's about mum," her father replied, "Now let's all sit down," and they sat.

"Your mother is very ill Sophie. She has been for a few months now. We haven't been sure how to tell you this because you don't have the context we do."

The word context set Sophie's mouth agape—"What does context have to with it? What are you talking about?"

"Sophie please, please just let me speak," Alastair said,

"Then get to the point!," Sophie cut in"!

"Right," Alastair continued tryingly:

"You don't know the context of your mother's current situation because you were too young to understand it at the time. Your mother was very, very ill after your birth and nearly died. No one really knew why but she did eventually get better, although she had to spend a good amount of your earliest years in hospitals. This all happened before you'd turned three and half, and your mother refused to talk about it after she returned home. Ed and John were old enough to work out what was going on and Arthur was old enough to ask questions about what he'd seen as a child, so we told him eventually. But you were too young to really see any of this, so you've never known. All this matters now because your mother is ill again. The sickness has come back, and while the doctors have assured us that they've developed a better understanding of what she suffers with since her last bout, they're a long way from anything resembling a full diagnosis. Frankly, we don't really know what's going to happen next … It's best you go and see her."

Sophie gazed at her father in a stunned silence. No words came out and no thoughts presented themselves, all there was only her father's morose expression. Everything surrounding that comforting face began to collapse into a blur and as the sharpness of the division starkened the world reached a deafening divergence. Sophie began to cry. Enormous tears flooded out of her eyes and hurt as they came. Her body convulsed and she had to ram her forearms down onto the table to steady herself as the they flowed. She felt her father's generous embrace around her and as he squeezed her tightly a wobbling, unconvincing, "It's going to be ok," troubled her ear.

Eventually Sophie's sobbing slowed and she pushed her father off. Standing up, she walked through the house towards the garden. There she kept walking. Sophie couldn't look at the furniture where they used to pass summer evenings, or the swings her siblings and parents would push her on. Past the fence she broke into a run, leaving it all behind, charging desperately towards the gate that led to the woods. Now at pace, she began to scream. Her cheeks burned as the wind tore at their salted redness. Flinging herself against the gate, she rolled to the right and threw it open behind her, running and running until the path turned to mud and the trees grew as densely behind her as in front of her. Only then was she able to stagger to a stop. Catching her breath, she lurched forward with hands supporting her on her knees as her had fell as blood and spit abseiled down her painful lips.

A little more collected now Sophie was able to raise herself up to the sun and bask in its rays as warmth and peace ran down her. Filled somehow, she rolled her head slowly left then then as her cheeks and arms repaired themselves from her flight. Finally she cupped her palms and let the heat dry them, ridding them brackish dowsing.

Chapter 12

Now drenched in soothing rays, Sophie set off wandering through the forest; bobbling from glade to glade in a trance, with each clearing opening itself up at the expense of everything that had gone before. These regular plunges took her deeper and deeper into the wild, with more being revealed every handful of steps. Sophie was in shock.

The woods weren't cleared this far in and so the corpses of uprooted pines lay all around her. Nature's bounty, they wrapped around her and their broken branches hung like flies trapped in a web. Cold and divorced from herself, Sophie pushed through her knotted surroundings letting more go with each step. The wounds became deeper. Yet she persevered—there was more to be torn away.

Practically entombed in the forest's tight grasp, Sophie crashed and crawled her way through it, crying as she went, one hand covering her face while the other cleared a path. Hot blood stung her eyes, and just as the burning became intolerable it collapsed into a numbing cool, blanketing her. This new plane bore her through branches which were now so thick that they resembled a knitted jumper. Finally she burst through into the light.

In a heap, almost comatose, cushioned by the grass of a clearing, Sophie rubbed her sweaty palms up and down all her limbs, scooping the blood into her quivering hands. In this state of confused devotion she raised herself to her knees and her gaze moved from her cupped hands to her surroundings. She was in a clearing dominated by an enormous oak tree. It was so large that its head almost met the edge of the surrounding forest, save for a foot that let in the circumambulating shaft of light that Sophie was now deposited in, and its roots drove out like the spiralling arms of a clock.

Sophie collapsed, set her bum on the backs of her heels, and sat back in awe. As she did so grappling vines touched her neck and grew upwards cradling her head and an almost completely depleted Sophie relaxed gratefully into their comforting embrace. As she gave in her surroundings grasped her more firmly; binding her wrists and forcing the created receptacle towards her now dipping head. In bringing these two statuesque elements together, like a superstructure restored, Sophie found herself drinking the contents of her elegant hands.

The warm draught invigorated her and on its completed consumption her palms slammed down to the ground. Sophie fell over herself and her mouth's fiery breath eviscerated the grass she landed on leaving only supple mud. Her ribs opened and closed and as her essence pumped up and down she throbbed with expectant pain. Aghast at her behaviour Sophie drew herself together and waited for the breath to shakily return. Distressed by what had just occurred, Sophie's mind span with thoughts at the forced imbibing. All this made her stomach slosh back and forth, gurgling its way through its newly ingested self and tearing at the surrounding lining like snakes in a sack—Sophie knelt in pain.

Rendered some withering succubus Sophie leapt up managed a few discombobulated steps before her flight was thwarted by that devouring beast. In fear she wilted and was once again downed, this time into the crook of one of the oak's great roots. She lay there in defeat, clutching her breasts in a futile attempt to nurture herself back to activity. Sophie's skin prickled as the vines came again—their progress could be felt iota by iota. This time they embalmed her in their enveloping reach and, finally exhausted and petrified, Sophie simply lay there. The appendages made their way up, cradling her head and swaddling her like a baby. Like great scooping parental hugs, they bore her like a pupae up and along the root towards its genus. At this central mass of nature Sophie was borne under one of her bearer's winking siblings and down into the murk. The stygian gloom momentarily stole everything from her surroundings. But once fulling submerged into this darkness she was raised anew into the warm innards of the oak.

Still an infant, Sophie was initially blinded by the veins of light that struck all around her through the suspended bark of the trunk. The scent of ambergris dominated the hollow so much so that it percolated out, like steam, through the same gaps which allowed the light to enter. The latter lit the former's exit like a fertile offering from above, and together this converse turned what might have been a cage into a wicker basket drifting on a river. All was inextricable from all. In this world there were only enlivening currents of excess given and bounties returned—abundance abounded. Yet this cycle was one of many, each a movement to a tide, and this tide simply washed over again and again with throbbing fertility. Sophie basked in her newfound world and the worries of her life fell away from her in front of her very eyes. Instead of an open wound this ridding left a sapling: a renewing definer of space, and paradoxically, an exchange.

It was in this state of abandon that a lavish voice visited her and began,

"Sophie, be free of yourself, now leave!" With this, a maxim as much as a dismissal, Sophie began to be rotated faster and faster until her surroundings turned to black. In this cyclone, she saw an old woman with wrinkled elbows and knocked knees smiling back across the void. The hag was made of twigs and her eyes were sallow with a yellow film. The rustic garb she wore hung formlessly around her and was bound at the waist by a furry belt. The former was patterned with yellow twine sewed in spirals through the whole piece, covering all the available space. As soon as she saw this figure Sophie's surroundings dissolved and she found herself planted in a loose pile of hay in the centre of a field of wild grass.

Sophie propped herself up and looked slowly from left to right in utter disbelief. The dream had been so vivid. She even had to check her arms and legs for scars—there were none.

Chapter 13

Sometime later Sophie awoke. The sky was streaked with pink and orange and Sophie realised that it must be getting on for evening. She rose, bones jangling, and lit a cigarette.

"Funny that," she thought to herself. On checking her phone and seeing she'd missed numerous calls from the boys she decided to wander back and put them all out of their misery.

"After all, I'm not dead and mum needs to be attended to. Besides, whatever's happened I can't fix it from the middle of a forest."

Sophie worked her way through these familiar reductions with a disconnected airiness as if there were a golden, if contrived, nugget of truth. This process, their computations, served the conclusion in so far as it obfuscated alternatives. And yet, this nugget—wasn't it the sun to the solar system that she was discovering for herself? These results were predictable, after all, she could look into her little something, and watch its mechanics work themselves through.

"Absurd really…"

This computing came to nothing. As the land fell away it suddenly devolved from a shallow curve into a progression of angled planes and returned upwards at the hill. It became stepped by its newly defined geometry. All at once, this badly modelled version of her surroundings broke itself into being all around her like blinds closing up all across the lands. An absurd image, as absurd as the dream, it had her standing mute, twisting and jerking, to catch all of its changes. As the insanity crescendoed once again all disappeared as immediately as it had come, and Sophie was once again left utterly dumbfounded.

Dimensionality was now restored. Yet golden threads snaked their way through the land like veins left in a dried riverbed; their resulting shimmer coating the land with effervescence— stardust left spreading in the wake of a charging comet.

Now truly disturbed Sophie hurried towards home disregarding what may or may not have happened, desperately focused on restoring some semblance of normality to her life. Sweating rivers and panting she eventually reached the front door and knocked her usual couple of thuds to allay the fears of her family. Alastair emerged breathlessly and an exhausted Sophie fell past him. She stumbled into the house and steadied herself against an abutting wall. Her chest heaved as the experience left her, and Alastair's expression was worried as he saw his daughter's eyes hollow to pools of stagnant memories. He wrapped his arms around Sophie, bending his enormous torso over her and holding her to him.

"Sophie I'm so relieved that you're back, we were worried sick, where did you go?"

To this paternal safety, Sophie gave herself; and she swooned, exhausted, sobbing as she went. Her head fell to the side and rested in the crook of her father's elbow as hot, baying, tears rolled out of her, drenching this sanctuary.

"Dad I need to see her, I need to see mum," she gasped. "I need to see her now, take me to the hospital, I can't bear waiting."

Alastair grimaced and his grip relaxed, brought back to the state of his dying wife.

"She had to see her, of course," he thought to himself. "But God why does she have to see her as she is now. What a horrible image to have of your mother before she dies."

"Yes, darling, we'll go now," he replied. "Clean yourself up. I'll get the car keys and tell the others, then we'll leave." He kissed his daughter, but his eyes remained raised, fixed on the image of his bedridden wife.

Sophie squeezed her father and freed herself from his embrace. In the kitchen, she found Arthur meekly poring over a paper. He raised his head and bit his lip as Sophie entered,

"I'm sorry Soph."

With this, his head fell once again. Sophie dried her eyes, gulped down a pint of water, and before turning towards the door glanced back at Arthur's dipped head and sighed. At the door she put on her coat and listened to her dad in the sitting room whispering something to the other two. Finished, Alastair came into view, they nodded at each other, and Sophie opened the door.

Together the pair drove towards town with the weather closing in as they went. Their journey took them from narrow, hedge-lined country lanes to roads that so awkward they might have been steamrollered accidentally through the wild land around and finally they found those roads of an English country town, with all their unconsidered irregularity. The air closed and the atmosphere thickened. Acidic rain accompanied the town's stickiness arresting Sophie and Alastair in their seats. Both had faces of grim dejection which only deepened when they were forced to close the open soft top and hunker in its relative safety. To Sophie the town was lumpy custard; unmistakeably English and totally unconsidered, with growths of Tudor, Victorian and Brutalist architecture. To her father, she knew, it was the depressing realisation of what he and her mother had been desperately trying to deny for the last thirty years.

Deep in the countryside, their local town was a hamlet. They'd seen the yearly change and generational incursion by "them." Them not being any people specifically, but those who viewed the countryside as a backward hangabout ripe for change. These movers and shakers were to Sophie's parents, like the brutalism they brought, pouring an obscuring cover on top of all the nuances that made their lives there. Most obvious of their machinations was the very hospital Sophie's mother was housed in at the moment. St Thomas' had been built in the sixties in the rubble of a munitions warehouse, and like its predecessor was one of the town's largest employers.

This was perhaps the saving grace in its detractors' eyes, Sophie pondered as they arrived at the grey car park under the grey sky of an overcast shower. Stilted, each made wry eyes at the other, commending one another on their decision to get coats. As they sat there wiggling and bumping up from their seats, Alastair reached a hand over to Sophie, covered her zip grasping hands with his palm, and squeezed. Sophie didn't know how to respond.

Chapter 14

Soon enough they left the car and toddled through the rain until they reached the shelter of the hospital proper.

"We're here to see Belinda Baker," Alastair said as they entered the bare hall.

"Go right on up," the face replied with a kindly nod.

There was a part of Sophie that quite liked hospitals—more the idea than the reality these days. Under different circumstances she would feel safe handing herself over to someone, and by extension something, that knew better.

But this was not one of those days, and indeed her mother wasn't in that situation.

This re-resignation to the circumstances had just settled as Sophie and her father rounded the doorframe and came face to face with her mother. She was lying in the crumpled hospital gown like a deflated balloon, wrinkled and skewwhiff. There was a strong odour which gave Sophie a headache, and it was in this dazed state that Sophie first looked down at her mother, who was capable of little more than a dull gaze. Belinda's normally coiffed hair was spread rattily over the pillow with stray stands hugging her face. Hands and arms withered with their veins pronounced and her body was flat and atrophied. Sophie's eyes moved from feature to feature, and yet the tears only came when she returned to her mother's pale, drawn face. Perhaps there had been too much to see and comprehend, but as her gaze settled on this ensoulment, her emotions were awakened and the air of resignation she held was transferred to her mother. Sophie finally felt herself to be seeing her mother as she truly was.

This thought horrified Sophie and she sharply dug her nails into her bare thighs as if to chastise herself. But she couldn't disagree with her realisation and, with the eyes of a vindicated coward, her gaze crept round towards her father. And there Sophie saw the face of utter despondency—its despair spilt out everywhere, it was crushing, Alastair's loneliness was palpable. There was a gulf between them, where one had never existed before: her father existed on an island that she didn't know how to reach.

"What does she have exactly," Sophie choked out.

"They didn't really know then and they don't really know now," Alastair replied, "It seems to be something to do with the lungs but I'm not sure they know at all. They kept questioning me about her smoking over and over again, as if asking the question in a different way would give a different answer. Fools," he spat this last word out. "They've run every test, jabbed her with every drip, and still her condition is deteriorating. They're dutiful, at least, but they seem to have consigned her to some mystery illness that is beyond their knowledge—it's absurd."

Sniffling, Sophie grabbed her father's hand and squeezed.

"I'm so sorry darling," her father sighed, "I should have told you sooner, I just didn't know how."

Sophie wept uncontrollably—something had revealed itself. Bending down she raised her father's palm and planted her forehead in his hand. Alastair duly wrapped his daughter up once again, rubbing her back slowly as he gazed at the various charts and diagrams along the hospital walls. All the blood vessels, organs and bones were there and yet here was his wife dying unaccountably before his eyes.

Sophie whimpered, the two embraced, and her mother began to let out a slow exhale. Belinda's lips parted revealing a set of small white teeth and a thick, parched, tongue.

"Alastair," she whispered, "Is that you?"

The words travelled towards the father and daughter like mist over cold glass. It was as if the tomb had been animated and the pair turned around aghast.

"Yes Billy it's me, and Sophie is here too."

"Oh, Sophie, darling, come here," Belinda replied.

Sophie obeyed and advanced awkwardly towards the head of the bed and seated herself on some of the ample empty space beside her mother. Belinda raised a withered arm, so stabbed with drips that it was like a pincushion, to caress Sophie's sticky cheeks.

"Oh, darling you've been crying, what for there's no need, you've no need to worry," Belinda continued. "Darling, take a tissue, there's one on the other side of me," she began again. "Go darling, go."

This was enough to raise Sophie from her stupor and as she left the bed her mother returned, satisfied, to her effigiac state.

Orders executed, Sophie looked down at her mother's silent frame and slowly dabbed her eyes with a quizzical expression, sniffing herself back to composure. Her father had taken her place next to her mother and Sophie was left a third party to this scene of holy matrimony. She preferred her mother in the idealised state she now saw her in. Here her mother was a vision of perfection and of a life well lived. There was medical equipment, yes, but in her silence it seemed to be merely stuck onto her rather than to be holding her. Belinda existed like a statuette ready to be raised for its adoration. Soon, it seemed, the stone masons would come, and her unfussed form would have completed its perilous journey through life perfectly.

Forced to hide, Sophie turned to the window.

Before her was an oppressively unrelenting grey. It began with the overcast sky and was cradled by the bare brutalist buildings; it was an unremitting deluge of the unconsidered facets of the world around her. The grey, which had once coloured the curtain leading to a new England, had become a dust sheet for any sort of cultural consideration. And now it lay still. It was into this desert that Sophie now felt herself sinking. These dunes enveloped her with the ease of an uninspired tide, inarguable in its utility and stagnant in its vision. This supreme averageness, and its complete enveloping, had latched to the "English nature," as certain continentals have called it. Together they had metastasised into a newly self-sabotaging identity for her country's people. Like a dagger to a floundering jester, desperate for its audience's return, its host had happily and hastily parted itself out, organ by organ, pound of flesh by pound of flesh, until only this sickly, yet pervertedly gleeful husk, remained.

At this Sophie shook her head heavily and turned around only to be greeted by her mother's gaze and pointing finger, it pushed her shoulders back, raised her chin; lifted her ribs and centred her gaze.

"Darling, how is London?" her mother enquired with surprising strength of tone.

"Oh, lovely, yes, it's all lots of fun," Sophie's reply came out in bits shrugged out like droppings from a rabbit.

"Oh good, I'm so glad, London is such fun"; assured of her progeny's direction, Belinda lowered herself to the bed and turned to her husband.

"Oh Alastair," she cooed.

And with that she relaxed back into herself and closed her eyes.

Her father dipped his head and kissed her mother softly on the forehead.

"She gets tired easily these days," he explained sorrowfully, "I'll leave you with her while I go to the loo."

Sophie nodded and looked back at her mother. She stood there waiting for thoughts to come to her, thoughts which would honour her mother and clarify her life during what might be their last meeting—but these thoughts did not come. She was left in a room with a dying woman, they were both cold, linked by a technicality.

Internally Sophie begged for her father to return and to remove her from this mortuary and let her back into her own world. There was nothing for her here, she thought to herself, and her dry eyes gave way to impatient huffing. She tapped her foot and slapped her thighs as her cheeks tightened and her pulse raced. Finally, unable to take it anymore, Sophie stormed out and went to find the gents so she could meet her dad on his way back. As she rounded a corner into the wing's main hall she bumped into a nurse who pointed her to the loos and asked if she was Belinda's daughter. "Yes," Sophie replied,

"Oh, I'm so sorry," the nurse replied, holding Sophie's hands in hers, "Take some time for yourself, you'll be ok."

At this accosting, however, Sophie was so disturbed that she practically pushed the well-meaning nurse out of the way. On her father's return, she asked that they drive home, and on the way Sophie explained that she was going back to London. Her father begged her to stay for a few hours but Sophie politely declined. When they crunched up the gravel drive she jumped out and went to collect her things for a swift goodbye.

Alastair stood in the doorway, distressed at the sight of his only daughter running away, but he had not the words to help her stay.

After Sophie's rapid organisation she gave each of the boys a cursory hug and strode outside towards the bus stop. It was only when she reached the sheltered seat and checked the time that her heart slowed and her breathing deepened. She saw a few inquiring messages from Daisy and, for the first time in a while, was relieved to be able to reply with lies about her life.

*

It was in this compelling state, on the train to London, that Sophie first saw *Ahriman's* work. Their presence was so au fait, in fact, that it was almost painful to scroll through the poetry and videography. Yet it bit like fresh rain on dry skin and succoured her with its life giving relief. The initial pain over her mother was now being carried towards a horizon that raced away as quickly as she approached. It must be like hitting terminal velocity, Sophie thought to herself, only the headwind soothed her rather than buffeting her.

Chapter 15

As the waves nudged him out of his flat and into his walk to the Dog and Duck, Max reviewed the previous few days. The photo shoots had been incredibly refreshing and his countenance bore a long missed balmy glow. Both had been indoors, with small groups of models, and focused on capturing aesthetics rather than their product. Max relished the unconsciousness with which he'd gone through the early shots, their opening up the room and defining the outfits had been extraordinarily satisfying. Once he'd found the nub of the project Max had joyfully begun to experiment with bending and twisting it in a bid to reveal the undercurrents more fully. While he hadn't previously met the actors their professionalism was obvious, and as the shoot went on they came together like parts of the same organism moving in compliment to one another. This groundwork, the ritualistic opening shots, and the amorphic models quieted participants' conscious minds, allowing their unconsciousnesses to flow out and fill the room. There, like underwater dancers, their movements took on an elegance impossible in the perverted air outside—together they gifted clarity. In the intervening evening, Max simply went home and slept. When Sunday evening finally came he bobbled down to his poker night and the evening began.

*

Whenever Max folded he'd sit back and enjoy the hands, played cards and gesticulations, fly around him accompanied by all sorts of swearing and insults. In these pockets of time his world slowed and he was able to consider the events of the previous couple of months—their irregular beats baffled him. Time seemed a slingshot, wound back during periods of intense and concentrated happenings. Only to go off and erase that part of itself which would have followed.

"If time were a string," he thought, "As some seemed to imply, it must be one that coiled at these points and unspooled in their aftermath."

Van Gogh's *Starry Night* came to mind, twinkling its promise at him. Through introspection to further introspection—it was draining. Max played what he had and re-joined game.

It was the same group as last time: Billy, Harry; Nick and Paul, and the conversation flowed. The middle two were enjoying the depth of their employment's groove, positing point and counterpoint in respect to their daily grind. Initially, Paul and Billy had interjected with vain attempts to wrap up the shop talk, but their sarky ribbons had been to no avail and Nick and Harry thundered on paying no notice to their friends democratising attempts. Despite their present floundering the wannabe arresters weren't doing badly, in real terms, compared to their friends. Both Paul and Billy had taken a step or two in carving out their own paths, and it was really their automatic self-deprecating that held them back from enjoyment—in more ways than one. Max could see their decisions claw at the backs of their minds and he laughed to himself at the ease of their suffering.

Eventually, however, enough alcohol had been consumed that even the ambitions of Nick and Harry were curbed, and the conversation finally turned to the customary ephemeral bollocks they all relished. This free for all all was a rejuvenating diversion from the noxious boredom of the real world. To the outsider, their linen shirts were chasubles, coloured pink as devotional proto-gammons, but they were too engrossed in real pleasure for such observations. Parry and riposte were the true delight of those evenings and yet somehow the thing fell a little askance and landed squarely in the black hole that was religion. All those involved had a vaguely CofE morality, or at least aspired to it. However, given that none were practising what this actually meant was fairly hard to deduce.

"… Well let's be honest none of us actually know the answer do we," Paul offered

"… Well no, I mean, at the end of the day it's no one else's business really," the weakness of this, Harry's reply, snagged on each's insides, causing pause. In a hurried attempt to patch up the gaping hole, Billy offered,

"Look it's not really part of any of our lives is it? I mean if we had a need or desire for it, it would be, and if it was then we'd have something to say here. So, you know…"

The reality of course, obvious to Max even more so now, was that none of them had anything close to enough of an understanding of Christianity to continue this conversation.

Max thought of *Ahriman* and all that had happened. His lizard like urge to flagellate himself in front of a priest and expunge his evil seemed as ridiculous as whatever *Ahriman* was,

"None of this is a priest's job, anyway," Max thought to himself.

The dilution of their Sunday social clubs rendered them mere purveyors of civil platitudes and unbounded abstractions which they no had intention of bringing to earth.

"No, this is visceral," Max thought, "This was where the fires of faith are formed—not desperately maintained—for the needs of the fewer and fewer."

Whatever *Ahriman*'s foil, then, it would be Max's to find and Max's to marshal.

The conversation moved on. Pints were knocked over and the game abandoned hand by hand until the group had settled into a euphoric bask under the warm night. Around twelve everyone dispersed preceded by wobbling hugs and grasping hands. They ambled their separate ways into the welcoming peace of their inebriated wanderings. Max too turned in the direction of his flat, and set off on his journey home.

Each step home brought him further into tune with himself and Max's inner settled into a comforting tempo. The world seemed to roll away from him, spinning a web between everything he could and couldn't see. With each step, this mycelium reformed around him, and he began to feel the expanse of himself—mind quieted, it flew out of itself, far away. This paradox, of immense movement and calm, was so mighty that Max found he couldn't be truly conscious of it lest he lose his grip on that which guided him forward. Instead it became the peripheral decoration for his subconsciousness, like mosaics—clarifying the space. Living was skimming this paradox as if it were a ridge and it was the realisation of this fact that induced a giving way to the revealing flickers of its unrationalized centre. Inner alignment was the raftsman tugging its way along the rope. Its touch on coarse palms promised infinite expansion, like the seam of a garment, it meant change and re-identification. And yet there was cognisance of some defining consistency. This through line, which was itself wrapped strings of determinable solidity, began behind him and continued after him and yet he was no strung maquette. He was himself the entire universe of possibility. Gauged now, his step increased and Max fired towards his flat barely aware of footfalls, and the fire within him devoured all that was him in perfect motion.

Yet as Max reached this ecstasy his guts tore themselves apart and a drooling, apoplectic *Ahriman* screamed as it emerged along with a deluge of choking soot. Its tail strangled Max and the host's pace slowed to a trudge, still forging forth he set about removing the constricting foe. The first attempt was a failure—*Ahriman* began to bite at the nape of his neck, tearing out bloody chunks out which strewed the path of its retreating victim. Max pressed on and he too bit his adversary, feeling the warm, dry flesh of his daemon's appendage. The result was a worm-eaten bruise, accompanied by the stench of its rot. In response *Ahriman* tore around and coming face to face with Max it bellowed:

"Arrest yourself, filth! Your clairvoyance lies to you and what you see is merely a fallacy for those who are puerile and weak. You must accept what you are and let it take you down so as to be reborn as you feel you should be," it sneered, "You are no soldier, no paragon of humanity with all its mythic baggage, you are the alpha and the omega, as you declare yourself so, and an act of yours will render you everything you have, can, and will be. Every aspect of yourself, all of humanity too, is bound up within this act and there is no world outside of it. You have felt within yourself something pertaining to a possibility, yet it is nothing more than the effervescence of the last choking bubbles of a once flowing spring!"

"No," Max retorted resoundingly. "I met Sophie. I have killed, yes, but I have loved and your fear of the latter causes you to split my axis for change in two, like the paltry reading you are, only to banish one from my mind—if that is not a final act of capitulation to the failures of your bilious prophesying then what is?"

Taken aback *Ahriman* bawled and Max continued,

"You are merely mine own outside of myself, my degeneration manifest. You are the creation of myself, the sum of my parts and as much subject to me as anything else of mine. I created you out of these, my sinning hands, and while you have purchase on my soul with each passing day you recede towards extinction. I see myself without you and realise you are but a cameraman to the race, feeding back what is, just as it becomes what it has been to everyone who doesn't decide what will be. But being beholden to you has run its course and I will cast you aside just as I cast you into being and banish you to the void."

At this climax, summoning all his strength for this fairy tale ending, Max was confronted by the empty river in all its tranquillity. His triumph. And yet *Ahriman* had disappeared. Max gazed over the peace in front of him and absentmindedly injected himself into the scene. He watched as his newfound surroundings rose and fell around him as he danced through their reforming with the assurance of unconsciousness. What had been a coliseum around him became the knowledge of courage and its burning manifestations all through all that there was. The expanse extended all around him, and his vision zoomed out further and further, only disturbed by firebreaks until eventually it became an inferno. This truly was everything that was all bound up in this undefinable mass of all that was and wasn't. The force of this realisation brought Max to his knees and when his sweating face rose he saw the remnants of this sun all around him. The glow of all that was emitted from the bank, the river, the houses, the pavement—an eternal colouring.

*

At home, sitting at his dining table, the colours of the room swelled around him and, swaddled by their embrace, their whispering sweetness tickled his ears. A couple of slow deep breaths, and despite all this the world around him seemed to be at peace.

Unfortunately, however, this bubble was burst by the driving ice pick of his realisation that *Ahriman* had been running, untethered, for days. Max hurriedly returned to his laptop and was confronted by a deluge of notifications across all platforms. He skimmed each and despaired at what was now dawning on him as an obvious resolution of his project. The legions of minecarts that together formed the trajectory of the self-perpetuating ecosystem that was his online presence had turned on him. One can map every possible interaction and still not produce conscience, so why would his mathematical attempt at identity development be any different? Max gazed at the screen like Nero over Rome, all was aflame, and all there was to do was watch. He had been turned on by the mob and now, apparently, he had to act.

It seemed, from a cursory exploration of his feeds, that the self-insulating world of his fandom had been broken, and a little perspective let in. A portion of those most involved in its creation had been exposed to one or more things that were outside their adorational lives, which had altered their experience of the world they had striven to create. The spell had been broken and the emperor had no clothes, or had the priests been caught manufacturing miracles? The spirit of the latter had begun to fast outweigh the former as anger turned to self-flagellation. Critiques of gesturing failures became indictments of the nature of the brand which turned to crying aspirations for future saviours. As *Ahriman's* digital rightening had fallen foul of its inability to accurately forecast society's crashing waves of narcissism, the burden of deified leadership was being re-posited as the mantle of an alternative digital face. As the teapot revolution wore on all of its parts were up for debate: the labels, the responsibility, the conversations. In short, all that had been codified and acknowledged as a part of the world, none of it was ephemeral. Not one of those prostrators before progress asked as to the nature of what was known. Instead, like blind bridgers, they continued to lay slats not looking where they'd end up or what they were passing over. Despite their experience beyond the looking glass, their foray was doomed and could only last a heartbeat before they were forced to leap back in and begin their building all over again. For if they, like Wiley Coyote, were ever removed from their cartoon world of narrative to be deposited in the world of action and life, they'd die a more real death than any they could possibly imagine.

Chapter 16

Sophie's Monday morning came like a hangover and stayed for the days that followed. Jason had returned to the office and was continuing his downward spiral for all to see. First came missed mornings, then missed days, then emails and phone calls started arriving at strange hours. His conduct had escalated enough for the powers that be to get involved, and after a few weeks, Jason was quietly given time off to allow them the breathing room to make a decision. It was this that had got Sophie to the Manchester hotel room where her feelings for Max bubbled away. They had been so intense at first. Sophie had wanted to throw herself into his arms, to be consumed by the patrician cultural affluence that his ilk suggested. There, in his familiar embrace, she could poke and pick at the walls surrounding her, only to giggle as they squeezed tighter. Oh to be succoured so, oh to enjoy her futile wriggling in response! In this emulsion she could finally be a figment of her own imagination, simply lost in the dark and unutterable forces that hurt so good.

However eventually this masochism began to fade and Sophie was left in a bereft state—yet she was bereft of something which she had never known. It burnt her deeply leaving a rough indentation, like a brand, of something that only apparently existed. Sophie was forced to struggle, clutching her stomach in pain, blind to that which would calm the storm.

Of course, with Max's absence and her feelings towards him cooling, she looked to others and imagined whether they would be able to fulfil her needs. This rawness begot self-destruction and she knew the catharsis of acid on an open wound. Yet each of these blows, in their tailor-made gloves, drove her further and further towards the edge of sanity. Each was a shuddering step taken backwards towards the edge of a cliff, the falling off of which would invite an endless descent of debatable delights into her life. And so she went round and round, striking and striking, hitting nothing but herself—let alone anything new. Repeated blows turned the bruises to wounds, and for each scab that formed another was torn off. Once again Sophie felt the directing pain showing her right back to that inescapable void.

No change of location, company, or activity could separate her from the drudgery of this continual barrage.

*

Two weeks later, still in London, Sophie got a call from her father.

"You need to come home now Sophie," Alastair sobbed down the line, "Sophie you need to come home—it's happened."

Just then Sophie saw how close she was to the cliff and, bloody-minded, she charged forward with bloodshot eyes and hurled herself off the edge,

"I can't," she blurted, mumbling something misheard down the line to her sobbing father.

Sophie hung up the phone and walked down into the kitchen. Daisy was there and Sophie sat down opposite her. Scenes like this haunted her as bookmarks of a life unchanged. Sophie didn't say a word, she simply had a glass of wine, and another, and then left.

Chapter 17

Steeled with understanding, Max began methodically removing *Ahriman* from the internet. Competitions, giveaways, and donations were honoured, much to everyone's surprise, and after that the accounts were left to themselves. Most followers would continue to produce take after take, unaware of his decision, and so he, the creator, finally had peace.

At this hour of convalescence, a knock came at the door and Max swung it open amiably to reveal a pair of luminescent policemen whose request to enter he answered with a subservient nod. He awkwardly directed them to the dining table and asked if they would like any tea, a request that was politely, but neutrally, declined. Max was bid to sit opposite them and there he steadied his lulling head in the palms of his hands.

"Thank you for letting us in Mr Hallam," the officer on the left began, "It's far easier to do this here than at the station. I'm Officer N'kimbo and this is Officer Richardson and we're here to ask you a few questions about someone you know—namely Mattew Tatterson. What can you tell us about him."

"Ah. I've heard," Max stammered, "Alex mentioned you wanted to talk to all of us … I'm afraid I have little to say, I only met him that night. I really don't know anything."

"Indulge us please," N'kimbo replied, "Let us worry about what there is to know," he continued, "Mr Nisbet assured me you'd all be cooperative, indeed everyone has been so far and I don't see why you shouldn't be. So if you would, we have a few questions.."

"Ok, yeah, I mean Alex's a good bloke," Max replied weakly, immediately chastising himself for saying something so pointless.

"Why don't you begin by telling us what happened the night you met Matthew, the night of the 16th" N'kimbo began, taking note of Max's mumbling.

"Well, I was going out, we met at a pub near Kensal Rise, so I took the tube there and arrived early evening—I really can't remember what time. Everyone was there and we all just had some pints and went from there." Colourless.

"And you met Sophie there for the first time, correct?" Richardson inquired.

"Yes," Max stammered, "And to be honest I stopped paying much attention to anything else after that point," he finished sheepishly.

"When you met her, you mean?"

"Yes," Max replied, refreshed, grateful for the escape. "I spent most of the evening with her and when she left I kicked around for a bit before heading off myself … Then I walked to the tube and went home," he shrugged.

"That's all?" asked N'kimbo.

"That's all" nodded Max.

"You haven't mentioned Mr Tatterson whatsoever,"

"He was there," Max stammered again, "He was just quite pissed so I didn't talk to him much."

"Did Mr Tatterson agitate anyone do you think? Did his inebriation get anyone's nerves?"

"Well I think we all found him a little annoying," Max retorted resentfully, "We left him behind for a reason." His exhortation was coloured with a tone of finality. Picking up on this, N'kimbo pressed him,

"How exactly was he annoying, Mr Hallam?"

"He was just getting in everyone's way, being a bit of a fucking tit, frankly."

N'kimbo betrayed a hint of amusement and asked directly,

"Was he getting in your way, Mr Hallam?" Max pulled back, reminding himself of what was at stake.

"Well, yes, every so often. As I said he was pretty pissed and the rest of us weren't, so it was just one of those situations really …"

"The problem is," began Richardson, "When people go missing for this long there's rarely a happy ending." The soft-spoken officer terrified Max and he suddenly felt completely out of his depth.

"So what we're really doing here is trying to ascertain what sort of unhappy end we should start looking into first," Richardson continued.

A chill ran all through Max's now sweating body. Overwhelmed, he was unable to disguise the shock and was on the verge of stammering something bordering on an admission, but N'kimbo came in just early enough to avoid collapse,

"You see the seriousness of the situation then Mr Hallam." N'kimbo's soothing allowed Max to turn his catatonic fear into shock and he panted out his emotions as proof of his familiarity with a sheltered life. His gaze rested on N'kimbo—he knew he couldn't trust his face under the stare of Richardson,

"I'm sorry," he replied, doe-eyed, "I hadn't looked at it that way. I don't remember anyone being so angry they'd do something about it if that's what you're asking."

"Do something about it," Richardson questioned.

"Well, you know what I mean, hurt him," he couldn't say kill. "Something that would lead to one of those unhappy endings you mentioned."

The officers let the silence hang in the air—it was as though Matt's corpse was suspended from the ceiling, and each was daring the other party to look up. The pressure was unbearable and Max, resisting, looked from one officer to another. Richardson cocked an eyebrow as their gazes met and N'kimbo leaned in, propping his frame on his elbows and touching his chin to his outstretched thumbs, and evenly asked,

"What do you think those unhappy endings might entail Max?" Chilled to the bone, a sharp intake of breath,

"Look I don't know, I'm just following your lead officers. This is all new to me" Max blurted back. The officers shared a smile,

"We have some more questions we'd like to ask you down at the station," Richardson stated.

Max seized the opportunity and sharpened his tone,

"Well if that's the case I'm calling a lawyer. End of." He raised his hands to indicate the reasonableness of his response. Neither officer changed his expression in reply to this, but Max was sure they felt they'd made a mistake with that question.

"Look there's no need for a lawyer," N'Kimbo replied simply.

"No, no," Max pressed, "Anything like that, anything in an interrogation room, and we aren't continuing this until I've got one—so that's that." Max's eyes were widely intense for just long enough for N'kimbo to reply,

"Alright, we'll be in touch."

The pair quietly got up and showed themselves out without any fuss,. Max was struck by his intelligence, he congratulated himself with an explanation of why he'd known to do that and how it had come from some hard-won experience. As he snickered to himself and continued his highlights reel of youthful run-ins with the Police the officers returned to their vehicle.

"He did it," Richardson stated simply.

"Mmmm," Nkimbo replied with a grimace, "Let's not jump to conclusions but yes, it looks likely."

"There's always something with this lot isn't there? Every one of them" Richardson said.

"Being a little highly strung might have something to do with that but yes I agree. Either way we need to look into him, if not just for more leverage," N'kimbo replied.

"Yeah, it'd be a laugh to start pulling up some of his past embarrassments and get him squirming," sneered Richardson,

"Yes, well," N'kimbo responded with staccato emotion, "There'll definitely be something we can dig up that'll worry him, and in the meantime, we can run his plates and requisition the others to see if we can create a fuller picture of Mr Hallam." The formality of this signing off amused Richardson a little and he nudged his senior. Giggling he added,

"Don't worry sir I don't think you're one of those."

*

As the police car drove away, its rubber tires crunching over the tarmac, Max startled awake from his incapacitating numbness. Did they know? He had no idea. He tried to work his way back through the encounter line by line but he couldn't. Max realised that whatever had happened meant that he had to be infinitely more careful and he definitely couldn't return to the grave, ever.

Yet he knew he had to confront himself somehow—the weight of his lack of perspective was wilting him. There was no easy answer and certainly no obvious beginning point for formulating a solution. Once again he was choking on his own emotions and drifting towards absolute inactivity. It was now, more than ever, that he surmised that he needed some sort of support. In this stupor Max was owned up to the crushing loneliness of the past few months. He had no one around him to lean on, not that he could gain empathy from those he did know, and he couldn't see much of a way to rectify this. Yet despite this, there was a glimmer of hope in the form of Sophie. Her perfection might inspire in him the nous to lay down the first plank in his path out of the bog. Better still she might simply raise him out of his mess by herself. The possibility of this mythic solution to his oh so temporal problem gratified him greatly, and it had him stroking his arms and purring like a cat. He must get in touch with her—all the memories they might create and all the trials and tribulations they might go through. How gleeful he was.

Chapter 18

Sophie's evening was one of savagery, of crashing through pubs and bars and forcing herself on the unsuspecting world. In the first, she got into some shots, flashed the rest of the bar, and heralded her exit by stealing a bottle of vodka. In the second, this bottle of vodka topped up her shots and became the fuel for a fire she started in the abutting alley. In the third, Sophie simply sailed in and offered to have sex with anyone interested. This provoked a confused, albeit positive response, and fifteen minutes later she was off to the fourth with a bottle of wine for her troubles.

Now very much worse for wear Sophie tried a final bar but her staggering entrance was blocked by a burly security guard. A dispute followed, with the latter's calm parrying garnering support from the punters, while the former's squawking grew. As Sophie's temper flared the wine bottle slipped into her grip like a club and the bouncer, catching this, drove her backwards, closing her down onto the cobbles. Only enraged by this, the fated bottle came up and endeavoured to bat away the man's retaliatory bear hug. Confident in his assailant's inebriation, the bouncer left an opening for a withdrawal despite the punches his palms received. Unfortunately this only served to allow the bottle to find its way behind his head and impact it showering glass and wine down his collar.

The bouncer fell in a heap, trapping Sophie's left leg under him. She sat up, dazed, and saw the bar's occupants gazing at her, and at the spasming body on top of her, in horror. The wound, pathetically caged by the victim's fingers coughed up blood by the glass—a geyser amongst the surrounding foliage. Sophie gazed at this burping little thing. All the noises died down and she was left with something that was beginning to look like a font in front of her. It sucked everything around it into negligence, like a vision. She was paralyzed by it and stood up, ruined, before the crowd.

Peace reigned only briefly before her fear tore it apart and Sophie fled with a drunken ferocity. Taking a left, then a right, she ended up in a rat run and continued on, taking whichever street was narrowest until she had lost herself in the lungs of the city. Yet this wasn't enough, she couldn't stay still. No dark corner could hold her; all were merely a sporadic respite from the immediacy of that image—the rocking gash and nothing quieted her mind against its ever resurging creep.

So, Sophie ran on and on until her legs couldn't hold. And yet on she hobbled with screaming thighs and shunting knees until the tears and sweat mixed into a paste between her skin and her shirt. It was only when the wind picked up and this glue chilled that Sophie slowed, wrapping her arms around herself and falling into a stumble that the haunting image caught up with her. As the street opened out in front of her the newfound space was filled by what she had done, projected for all to see. On Sophie walked, she was overwhelmed and worried that the window's occupants would wake and see what was in front of them—it was inescapable. There was nowhere to run and nothing to shield her.

As the pain became intolerable Sophie's feet found the welcome softness of mud and grass underfoot. Her sore, blistered feet were unshod and she knurled them into the damp balm beneath. As she padded forward the odd blade tickled her swollen feet and Sophie sat down to massage them back to health. Cross-legged, she worked her thumbs into her soles allowing the fat to return and the blood to dissipate. Calmer, she did the same to her calves and then her thighs, working her way up her body until she finished with her neck. To befit this newborn state she took off her clothes and stood before herself, naked, noticing that in front of her was a copse of thickly leaved trees obscuring what lay inside.

The hallowed space in front of her appeared as some underlying reality usually obscured by the metropolitan layers atop. Its trunks and branches knotted back and forth weaving a web ripe for a hero to cut through. And so, atop the crest of a wave so mighty it was visible only to the straining's of her mind's eye, Sophie walked towards the trees. Now was the crash. She would be thrown—how far she knew not. She only knew that the wash's high water mark was a cusp over which lay a forceful aridity.

Advancing, Sophie reached the first rough bark and ran her fingers along the deep fissures, feeling each piece's age. She tried to force her body through the outermost wrapped trees, but she was unable to; too tight, they repelled her supple flesh. Enraged at her weakness Sophie tore at the bark only to cover her fingers in its viscous sap. Furious, Sophie rubbed them along her naked arm feeling like a fool exposed to the elements.

Yet the sap spread like treacle, slowly covering her body. Sophie slicked herself with more and more until a protective layer formed over her puckered flesh and she was able to re-attempt her first obstacle. Crawling in blind, relying on touch and the wave that pushed her so violently forward—each new branch gifted her more sap which she gratefully accepted, even swallowing some to slake her risen thirst. No longer parched, within or without, Sophie passed through the trees like a fish through coral and emerged anew on the other side.

Before her the unknown spoke with familiarity to her adjusting eyes, and when she was able to see again Sophie realised she was in a clearing with a tree at the centre. Its roots emerged like spokes and vines covered it from head to toe.

At her entrance they began to crawl towards Sophie snaking forwards with ease and purpose, unneeding of the parlour tricks they had employed previously. In response Sophie stood at ease with herself, confident in the wave's tactile assurance of her place, and waited for the vines' arrival. And so, they, the omniscient and the omnipresent met with the quiet understanding of a predestination known. Nothing was said. The mass peeled itself away to reveal a flame, dancing as if it were Prometheus' own. It glided into Sophie's mouth, passed down her throat; continued to her stomach and settled in her loins. There it warmed the stagnant sap inside, thickening it, and producing a fibrousness that filled her body with strength and resolve.

Now metamorphosised, the crying voice within her was silent, and the screaming void was satiated with fire-formed mana. This fullness of self stood her up tall, and like a living statue Sophie found actuality. Her fruits flourished and Sophie bled. A mighty storm whipped up in the sanctuary and its rising eye seized her and raised her out of the copse. Inside, Sophie flew through the spiralling tunnel produced between her spine and cerebellum. Her memories, both bodily and psychological, were torn into view and Sophie coursed between the packed walls they created. All that had been and still was became simply those things that are. The eye drew all within its gaze back into itself and the storm collapsed, depositing Sophie in the middle of the park.

Chapter 19

Returned. Now lying under the stretched stars, Sophie no longer saw waves and crescendos but cycling peaks and troughs.

"What would become of this stillness," she wondered, "Forgiveness and repair would be championed," she thought to herself—and yet the allusion to some torn blanket lingered uncomfortably.

Oddly, her flight would be forgiven—Sophie was sure of it. The extreme reaction was to an extreme scenario; allowances would be made. It was the work, however, that would commence after the ritualised slapping and joking that would grind and scream. Fast-turning wheels of good greasing would have to be slowed, and their course changed.

This clairvoyance, however, left a pang of worry at its retreat. What could begin as a repairing could become a mediation and that, surely, was not to be her role? After all, to be the frame around which patterns were stitched seemed to denigrate her purpose substantially. If she was to be the healing force Sophie felt herself to be, she must be more than some inanimate binding agent. Sophie decided she had to circle herself—lunarly.

Sophie thought of the vines and how they revealed the fallacy of her omnipresence. Settling, she laughed to herself,

"That belly laugh" Sophie giggled, "I don't think a sound like that has ever come out of me."

Touched by the absurdity and its freshness in the air, a delightful unfamiliarity shelled her orb of vision.

This new path she was treading, Sophie only knew footfall by footfall, but it was undoubtedly her own. Thoughts of Daisy and Jason came with a sighing deflation; the former being who she now decidedly wasn't, and the latter who, until recently, she could well have become. And before her was the start and finish line of a race she was barely fit enough to run.

The next morning Sophie called in sick and then spoke to her father, explaining she was coming home. Alastair's relief breathed down the phone and Sophie's excitement rallied as she began to pack. Nerves banged their way back up again. Little could be done, Sophie decided as she left for Paddington, decrying her head's primacy over her heart.

*

A sympathetic Arthur met her at the station. He smiled sappily and rubbed her head affectionately, just as he had as a child.

"Arthur, I'm sorry for running away,"

"Oh don't worry," he brushed back, hastily, "Totally understandable."

"No, you must understand, I'm sorry,"

"Sophie…," Arthur croaked back, questioning this acquiesence.

"Yet to give is to win," Sophie thought to herself. Something her mother hadn't expressed so well. "The process of exchange is perhaps best begun by those who took the most?"

*

The pair passed through the blessed countryside, and as they neared their house Arthur glanced warily at his sister. The unsaid lay heavily between them and as the car ground to a halt on their gravel drive she began,

"Arthur, I shouldn't have run. Not least because I have things I'll need to say but because we will all have things we need to say."

The pontification of this would have struck Arthur if it didn't fall so instep with the absurdity of her actions the last time she was here. Sophie, dissatisfied with the inelegance of her beginning, paused to wait for some interjection, but her brother simply stared back at her mutely.

"Arthur," Sophie continued, "I'm utterly spun out, I can't be anywhere."

Each word came, evenly beaten, out of her full lips. With these fuller phrases Sophie was slow walking both Arthur and herself, to some, still invisible, conclusion ahead.

"Ok," came the reply, and Sophie squeezed Arthur's wrist and got out of the car.

Together the siblings entered and Arthur announced their arrival,

"Sophie's home … They're in there," he continued as he looked at his sister with awkwardly affectionate eyes. Sophie found the rest of her family standing about the dining room as before, the war room as she sometimes jokingly referred to it. Alastair wrapped her up once again in his bear hug and Sophie accepted but removed herself at the earliest opportunity. She looked at her family and saw listlessness spooled out on the floor like abandoned knitting.

"When's the funeral?" Sophie asked.

"A week on Sunday." came the reply.

"How far have you got with organising it?" she continued,

"A little way, but lots to go." A staccato exchange, as if they were swapping the parts of some flat-pack furniture.

*

Later, back in her room, Sophie thought of her mother. She remembered her directing the weeding and instilling the facts of presentation. There in mind no doubt, but in body? But her body? The maternal passivity that Sophie had draped herself over as a child was something uninhabited, it was merely something Sophie operated around—that seemed a gift given by her mother.

Leaning back against the wall, Sophie looked around her room and thought about all that was around her here and at her flat. Everywhere were shorthands for a life understood and all were ready to be given to another. Yet in the copse Sophie had seen an alternative. There, the vines, grass, saplings, roots, and trees weren't objects placed around her to please her. They all grew outwards through themselves; an extension of the existential—something real. Sophie knew the force was inside of her too; planted like a seed in that void that had so consumed her before. Yet it was no desperate plugging; it created itself to be the centre of what surrounded it, the giver of what its encompassers needed. This burly thought forced itself to the surface like the roots of the tree she had so briefly been imprisoned in. It was the turgid centre of what would come to be. It was strange, Sophie thought,

"What had for so long been a process of arranging the readymade has become a process of inhabiting that which grew."

Chapter 20

There was little progress to be made that evening—little said, little asked. Yet at dinner Sophie unexpectedly enjoyed her food, glancing neither left or right. The others didn't know what to make of the youngest's composure. In fact her unaffected sincerity yielded quite an exchange between their gazes.

And so the evening turned to night and Sophie lay in bed drifting in and out of sleep. Bored, she turned over and found *Ahriman* again. Sophie was amazed at how much it had grown in popularity—it had even impregnated the mainstream. She was equally amazed at the dissent within its follower base. The madness of it all baffled her and Sophie wondered what *Ahriman* himself must feel about this. Not exactly her bag, its cold touch felt reminiscent of her life in London.

At this, Sophie began to lament her own storytelling and realised that she had fallen into same the trap of believing her own myth. When she did return and rejoin the rush, would the great friezes she'd erected still be? No, they'd no doubt be smashed in the rapids of her river's broken meandering. So where was she? Sophie was perhaps on the verge of being able to let go, to let it all slip through her fingers and abandon it to itself. And allowing her to be reborn anew.

The morning brought the family down to breakfast and back to their stilted interactions. Over the next few days they kept to their general routine: breakfast, separate, lunch, separate, and supper followed by an evening spent loosely together. Sophie did little: she initially busied herself with some of the domestic chores but after completing them quickly moved on to freshening the rest of the house.

Each left the others largely to themselves and barring some superficial conversations, each was allowed their own space to mourn. Sophie completed her revitalizing and continued to beautify and create new life in the house. In a bid to bring the house together she began to design a wand to be placed on the dining room table: a symbol of remembrance for her mother. Each day Sophie went into town for more materials, allowing the artwork to create itself incrementally. Her brothers were confused by this pattern of buying, but it wasn't for them to understand.

Sophie was sure it was something meant to be held and given, but that was as far as it allowed itself to be envisioned. The shape grew over the following days, becoming something that lay softly in the palm. It wasn't a cross or anything rigid, nothing devotional that might serve as a rod against which to act out their sadness. Instead it was tactile with suggestive undulations; allowing one thought to flow into another. One's hands could walk around and around it as if they were exploring a Mobius strip. It took the user to infinity, palm by palm, and with each clasp that which was constricted relaxed a little more.

When creating this amorphous object Sophie sat askance in the war room with her bare feet and painted toenails propped up on the table. There, without a care in the world, she slowly knitted, stitched, pressed, moulded and carved her work. As it grew and Sophie's presence in the dining room began to be counted on, the rest of her family took an interest in what she was doing. Her brothers, in particular, would pop their heads in and shoot a few dismissive questions at her. She replied with equanimity, keeping focus on her work. Alastair came in too and he looked at her with an unfamiliar eye that asked where from rather than why.

Sophie diligently continued until Saturday when the weather broke and gave them a summer shower. She drew her work to a close, sitting her creation in the middle of the dining room table. She got up and walked outside into the rain, and it was under this deluge that the tension and closeness of the previous week was finally washed away, leaving Sophie cleansed, refreshed, and joyous.

After supper she went upstairs, leaving her family to discuss her addition to the house. Lying in her bed, Sophie checked back on *Ahriman*, and watched the unwinding gain pace. The infighting within the already splintered community had spilled over and was being collected and directed towards *Ahriman* itself.

"So many metaphors and all of them wasted on yet another insouciant attempt at a valuable contribution," Sophie thought to herself.

She wondered what it must be like being one of these influencers, scrabbling for enough shards of glass to throw up into the light—an image only for the briefest moment. She was further saddened by her own lesser attempts at the same. It was only last night that she had shed this skin, however, and she decided she must bolt the door on that life forever.

Bursting downstairs Sophie found the war room filled with her remaining family. They were sitting around the table, drinks in hand, looking at her creation. On her entry, Ed turned and asked with a surprising curiosity,

"Sophie, what's that?" While the rest of the gawkers turned and gazed at her expectantly Sophie replied, "I made it for mum."

Irritated at her lazy obfuscating Sophie started again,

"I kneaded my feelings about mum's passing into it. You can take it and feel what I've felt, you can give your own to it and give it to someone else. I thought it would help me, and maybe it will help you too."

At this Alastair threw back his chair and exploded,

"How dare you play the fool at a time like this after you ran away. You were meant to be here, present, and now that you're back you're offering us some sort of feeling stick? What the hell do you think you're doing?"

The words ricocheted around the room as he stood, rosacea flared, eyes narrowed and posture rigid. A thick finger was pointed towards Sophie like a gun, but as his booming words sparked from wall to wall she returned his gaze with fibrous intent. Her brothers were shocked but all stayed seated as the battle thickened over them.

"Dad I haven't asked you to do anything and I'm not going to. I made this for me, please calm down. I don't know what to do with myself now that mum's gone. I don't want to go back to work and I'm not sure I can. I want to be here with you, but I don't know how to. Everything I've got to go back to seems immaterial—it doesn't seem to mean anything but I don't know what else to do. I loved Mum as she raised us to love her—from afar. That doesn't mean to say I didn't know her, I did, I'm just not sure she knew herself, and I think she passed that down to me. I have no idea what to do. I can't just go through the motions. I can't just walk into a church and have everything wrapped up in speeches and sermons. I need more."

"Well it's not about you, it's about her," Ed cut in, but Sophie barged on,

"Obviously, but we're the ones doing the damn mourning and putting everything together for the funeral. If she's to be carried in our memories, she has to have been reborn in our minds and her spirit allowed to cleanse itself of that which we keep her unfairly welded to ourselves with.

"Am I making sense?" she exclaimed with jerking motions. "Enough," Alastair replied in a rueful tone.

Chapter 21

The next morning Sophie took her leave and went back to London to sort out what she'd left behind. She hugged all the boys tightly, especially her father who gave her a squeeze and offered to drive her to the station. In the car they sat in silence, and it was only when they parked up in front of the station that Alastair was able to bring himself to speak.

"Mum wasn't perfect, but she was a good mother. Perhaps, as you said, the way she was makes the grief harder, but things don't work like they used to…," He trailed on, "What else is there to do but sally on—if that's in silence then so be it. At least one doesn't have to bear witness to the horror. You must understand that there were systems, nuances, and affectations to help us through times like this. Your mother was nothing if not an exemplar of that way of living. Elegant and refined, she spoke to something larger than herself, to the intangible, to something even less perceptible to me than you these days. We didn't manage to pass that along and that's our fault. But you, you lot, you demand so much sincerity! But you don't really understand what it means. I used to think it was some factor of youth, but it seems to be a factor of society."

Sophie nodded, "But if life is just an assemblage of things that get you through, then why keep going?" she asked softly. "Isn't it better to bow to something larger than yourself on the principle that it'll give you more than you know, rather than trudging forward and stooping lower and lower to leave the snags behind?"

"Bowing and stooping—what's the difference?" Alastair asked.

"Well at least the former assures that one will get back up … I'll see you soon." With that, Sophie turned and headed back to London.

*

It was midday when Sophie arrived home, and Daisy was slumped over the dining table. She was still in her something dressy from the night before, but the glass of white next to her had spoiled into a vinegary scent.

Sophie perched on the edge of her table and stroked her housemate's hair behind her ear, listening to her light snoring,

"Ends were beginning for others too," she thought. "Nothing physical, or necessarily final, but relationships were being established and potentialities extinguished. People had decided their lives, for the time being at least. It does seem so damning said like that," Sophie thought.

Upstairs, Sophie smirked as the words 'Feng Shui' flashed across her mind. She sorted through her clothes and knickknacks with an easy pace and assured eye; she wasn't in a rush. Daisy would sleep on and Sophie would be left to her cleaning.

She'd rent the room out, Sophie thought, as her gaze fell on Daisy once again,

"Overlapping superficialities," she mumbled to herself.

Sophie bore Daisy no ill will though, and as was likely quite normal, they had grown apart for reasons which had nothing to do with one another. However, a thought struck her—she had never seen Daisy's room. Daisy had seen hers once or twice but she never seen Daisy's. So, in a final gesture, Sophie walked towards her housemate's door and opened it to discover what she was leaving. Inside was just a bare room with clumps of clothes shoved into corners. It was sparsely furnished and its white, functional occupants had been dirtied by Daisy's daily haste and by a low level stank which walked its clawing fingers up Sophie's nose and stung her eyes. The blind was down and the bright daylight, a three-sided square, gave the room an abandoned feel—it was terrible to see. This is what Daisy's striving had got her: a room with a lock that she daren't spend any time in lest her life left her behind.

And Daisy really could do anything she wanted—yet all she did was what she had been told to want. She was one of a faceless many ordered to march to where she did not know, and with each step a blind assurance took her down the path and to the advancing cliff edge. Max seemed to have something of that, it occurred to her suddenly, and Sophie wondered if he saw someone like Daisy as she saw him. Max was smart enough to understand, if she explained what she thought to him, but from the outset he'd miss the wood for the trees. He'd see the smudges of last week's makeup and guess the Vogue-directed flower arrangement. He could make a few lunging statements about Daisy being a product of a time and a place that they both knew. It would be a wink, wink, nudge, nudge, kind of statement, one that relied on Sophie's belief to not to question him further about what was driving at. He would be content enough to drift through life notching where he could, hopping from one upwardly moving belt to the next and ascending the Grand Staircase that he'd read so much about as a child.

Sophie finished clearing her room after that.

*

It was only when she was in the cab thundering along the M25 that she realised she hadn't left Daisy a note, or anything to explain what she was doing,

"Too bad," Sophie said to herself, "I'll have a better idea of what I am actually doing by the time she thinks to call."

Internal freedom. No doubt the snagging trappings of modernity would regain their purchase at some point in the future, but Sophie would deal with them as and when they came. She knew she wouldn't miss her work friends, they couldn't have had a more transactional relationship if they'd been paying each other. The set activities they participated in didn't bind them, and all their absurd desires to self-identify as parts gave them a usefulness to mould, not a personality to enjoy.

Finally, as Sophie rolled her way to a stop on the gravel drive next to the Mini, she thought back to her experience in the woods. It had altered every fibre of her being, she knew that. But, as a change carried through her, she was only aware of her new bearing, and was without signposts that could direct her back. Sophie sat in her cab and pondered this while she smoked a cigarette. She knew less than she did about her life before all this happened. She was now so far away from that exhibition, that the version of her who had grumbled her way through the preparations day after day, for however long, seemed to be someone else's memory. Sophie wasn't sure if she would ever leave that copse now. It felt like her centre and whatever came next would presumably be a challenge borne through this connection. Her previous life had tied itself off from her like a finished tapestry and her journey continued. Would the view back over her shoulder become more acute with each passing day? There was a part of her which was saddened by this: so many things had been lost—but what were they? They had drifted away like an overcast morning; a masking gloom devoid of discernible nuance which was perhaps best left behind.

As she took her final drag her phone bleeped, Sophie flicked the cigarette and looked at the glass slab tucked in her cup holder. In it was an email,

"Dear All,

We are sorry to inform you of Jason's passing. He was found two days ago in his flat after he had not been heard from for two weeks. The circumstances of his death are not known at the moment, but the news has been passed on to his family. Jason was a valued member of the team and we will miss him greatly. There will be an upcoming announcement regarding his funeral and remembrance.

During this intermediary period we wanted to give our deepest condolences for what has been a terrible loss, especially to you, his team."

Chapter 22

Wearily, Max forced eyes fully open, biting the insides of his cheeks in a bid to stay awake. Under protective arms his head continued to swing left and he found himself looking back at him with his eyes twinkling despite his drawn features. It was a pleasant surprise. Returning along its path Max found himself opposite a bare grey wall, a single continuous surface, which had, no doubt, served as a canvas for the warped thoughts of the many that had gone before him.

The last week had been uneventful. Sophie still hadn't replied (treading water came to mind) and Max was embarrassed that despite his longing only an impression of her face remained. She seemed a spectre now, more of a guiding spirit, that, with a beckoning hand drew him out of himself—only joinable on his recognition of the revelation. Yet how comforting, Max thought to himself, that he was able to know the unknowable and to be the pursuer of this redemptive shade through the labyrinth. This flitting fairy danced before him, transfixing him, and just as she turned to lay her lashed eyes upon him, the door behind her swung open backwards. She flew, only to be replaced by two incoming figures from out in the corridor.

Officers N'kimbo and Richardson came forth, each with a slim folder, and lumbered into the opposite chairs letting their jackets settle around them.

"Thanks for coming in Max," N'kimbo began warmly, "As was explained over the phone this is another informal interview about the disappearance of Mr Tatterson,"

Max cut in, "Please, Mr N'kimbo I'm waiting for my lawyer."

N'kimbo cleared his throat with a smile and continued, "Max as I said this is as equally informal chat as the last and you are welcome to a lawyer but it really isn't necessary." His smoothness was beginning to bite.

"So equally informal that I'm in an interrogation room rather than my kitchen," Max cut back.

"And are there degrees of equality Max," N'kimbo retorted teasingly.

The leading question caused Max to beat a meek retreat in sudden awareness of his lack of footing. Luckily, however, he was replaced on the front by his lawyer who burst in brandishing a briefcase and a cup of tea.

"Right, Right—, that's quite enough of that. Max shut up . Officers, what can I do for you?" the voice bellowed. N'kimbo, occupied with sucking his teeth and rolling his eyes at the new entrant, missed Richardson shooting Max a gruesome tormenting stare.

"I am Mr Valentine," the lawyer introduced himself, "And you are?"

"Officers N'kimbo and Richardson," N'kimbo replied gesturing to himself and to his partner in turn.

"Right," Valentine barged on, "You can consider anything my client said before now null and void, let's begin anew," he smiled.

"Right," N'kimbo ruffled his stack and hissed, almost to himself,

"Max we are interviewing you about the disappearance of Matthew Tatterson. Since our last interview new evidence has come to light and we require your thoughts on the matter…."

"What evidence might this be?" Valentine jibed. "Evidence regarding the possible moving of his body?" But before the officer could reply Valentine cut in again, tearing the hanging statement out of the air and smashing it on the concrete below;

"What the hell does that mean N'Kimbo—we don't know there's a body and we don't know where it might have been found. We don't know where it's gone and we don't know what could be even remotely evidential about your findings."

More than a little taken aback by this outburst, N'kimbo marshalled himself but before he could riposte Richardson hurled himself into the fray,

"Now why don't you let us do our jobs and you'll find out, you…,"

"Oh how very cops and robbers of you, what was your name then? I'll direct you towards the nearest cutpurse," Valentine cut in again. Richardson's brief confusion turned to rage and the steam flooding out his ears choked N'kimbo to silence.

"Go on then Officer Richardson, why don't you lay out your story so that my client can have a fair shake," Valentine continued, glancing at Max.

It only really dawned on Max then that he hadn't a clue who this man was. The middle aged ex rugby type sitting next to him had strong features obscured with a chortling filling of well spread fat. His lips puckered out perfectly to fit a port glass, and his gammon like palms looked were actifit holds for pints of stout. He was Jermyn-Street-And-Worn from top to toe and Max found it quite refreshing to see someone whose conception of an office didn't involve the phrase, "let's circle back." And so, a little overwhelmed, Max leaned back to watch the ensuing pantomime.

N'kimbo, regaining himself intermittently, remained mostly on the ropes, put there by some outburst from one of the others. Something of an academic horror lay behind the officer's befuddled eyes on witnessing the slugging match before him. Richardson and Valentine, both unacademic by existence, were performing a dance of courtroom ribaldry—very much Crown Prosecution Service versus Prosecuted Crown Service. Richardson, having now completely lost his cool, screamed back at the equally apoplectic Valentine,

"Oh there it is you posh bastard, the sky'll fall before you do things by the book, won't it?"

"Well, what do you expect me to do when the book is wielded by as perfidious a whack-a-mole player as you?" Valentine replied. Battle lines drawn, the final stalemate assured each that the other was the opposite side of the same coin that they both so highly prized. Neither was willing to give an inch, and so something on the outside would have to.

*

The meeting adjourned with N'kimbo still invalided, and so Valentine and Max showed themselves out and into the blinding sun on Charing Cross. Max turned back to Valentine, his neck twisted against the sun and he was a little spellbound by the man before him. Valentine had thick wavy hair and a great jolly beard, all grey. He wore thick rectangular glasses and had the balled up wrapper of a pork pie in his right hand,

"Come on," the older man thrashed, "Let's get some lunch."

Max followed his step obediently and as they strode through central London he found his gaze hopping from cornice, to balustrade, and to column with a refreshing alacrity. Here, he always felt, was something on the peripheries of his mind that could guide him forward. Again, Max thought of Sophie and checked his phone to no avail.

Rounding the corner into a cobblestone alley, Valentine jerked Max through a Tudor doorway and led him into a pub. It was low ceilinged, dark wooded and brown on brown. Max was escorted to the far corner where Valentine heaved himself into an enclosed booth where gargoyles were carved on the shoulders of each bench.

"I thought that went rather well," Valentine began bemusedly, "They don't have much—you're likely the only tree they have to shake, I reckon."

Shrivelling up at the prospect of what this man may or may not know, Max stammered back,

"I'm afraid I have no idea who you are, Sir," he gulped back.

"Apart from your lawyer," Valentine replied mockingly.

"Yes, but," Max's head swam and he grimaced, "I wasn't sure you were actually coming."

"Yes, a tearful reality in our current justice system, I grant you, but nonetheless I am here! And I am here to help you," Valentine continued in a truncated and wobbling tone. "Look, Richardson is the one to worry about, N'kimbo doesn't have the balls for scrapping but he does."

"And? And what about the fucking evidence!" Max replied hoarsly.

"They have none," Valentine replied firmly. "They don't have any because they didn't investigate quickly or thoroughly enough. I'll bet everything they might have had has been lost, either destroyed by the rain, or obfuscated by the tramplings of our Londoners. Admittedly, there may be some circumstantial CCTV evidence, but there's no bodycam footage—which is what really matters, and, frankly, you'd be surprised at what little can be done with the former."

"So, am I in the clear, will they drop the charges?"

"Eventually, yes," Valentine continued, "But for a while they'll hound you—until they're forced to move on. You need to sit tight and wait."

Here Valentine stopped the conversation and ordered himself a steak and kidney pie and Max a burger. The former ate with the ferocity of someone with far less circumference, while the other merely tapped his brioche bun with a thoughtful rhythm. The question that had been bubbling in Max's mind for so long that it was now painful to ask was an obvious one: who was paying Valentine and how much knowledge did the man have of what had actually happened? Was there some wallet of the defendable, some guardian of the innocent? The man's temperament was jolly, Max thought to himself, he seemed to have his mind made up about the case and he was certainly unfussed by its crux.

It interested Max that he was so occupied with the personalities of the two officers, but then with all the potential evidence apparently unsalvageable, the whole thing did become something of a zero sum game. Or was this how it had always been, Max wondered. It had been a performance after all—there were necessary parts. Decidedly, however, one thing Max was sure of was that these dimensions playing over a flat base was far preferable to a fight amongst the columns of yesteryear.

The bare room and the police station's Brutalist exterior returned to him. Whatever was out here, whatever was real, would surely die in there, and God only knows what would happen if one could never leave.

Valentine finished his meal and cleansed the room with a resounding burp, he wiped the pie scrapings off either side of his cheeks and leaned forward on his elbows. At this Max duly shrank back into his chair and had to force a forward jerk back to meet the man. The latter flicked his eyes up and down his client,

"You seem to think somebody's paying me, don't you?"

"Yes," Max's rattled brain calmed.

"No one's paying me," Valentine replied with an almost wistful exhale,

"In fact," pointing a fat finger at Max, "You're the last who won't. You're my last case for the bar, this is my last hurrah for the Crown," he shook his head and his eyes fell inward,

"Bit of a sizzler then, for my last ride, I suppose."

"I'm sorry," Max replied, "What does this have to do with me?"

"I chose to take your case you idiot," Valentine replied. "I thought, why not? It seemed to be about all the right things and I thought it would give me something to remember this malarky by, despite what it's all become…," Realising that Max was clueless as to what he was talking about, Valentine returned to the case, "Look, from the Police's perspective the goal of that interview was to scare you in the hope you'd reveal something minor which they could use to hold you. But they failed, and now they're under even more pressure to develop some sort of fuller picture to present to their superiors. But, as I said, they don't have anything and now they're looking for reasons to question you further down the line. Yours truly has stopped that, however, and now we are where we are."

"Thank God for the state," Max replied, winded,

"And you did all this of your own volition and your own discretion?"

"Yes," Valentine replied jovially, stretching his arms to their fullest, his suit almost ripping.

"Well thank you!" Max replied with a sort of abrupt gratitude.

"Well, of course," replied Valentine with shining eyes and a banana grin.

"Well best be off, I'll see you soon. Stay out of trouble 'til then." He forced himself out of the booth and turned for a deep wave and a bow.

Max sat dumbstruck in the booth as he watched his saviour's rotund figure exiting the pub. The events of the morning washed back,

"All these punters," he thought. The inner-city lunchtime crowd was truly prehistoric now, and yet the few pints, cheques and portraits that remained brought together enough of a flavour that the memory limply remained." Max's mind returned to his lawyer and the officer's back and forth. N'kimbo's entry to the fold came from somewhere quite different, somewhere more familiar if he was to be honest with himself.

"I suppose he was right to have me coaxably placed under his conscientious eye."

The ground the other two had fought over didn't exist anymore—that much was clear from Valentine's wistfulness and presumably why he was going private. This for the modern Rumpole—the man seemed practically born for a wig and a cigar. Max did feel oddly safe under Valentine; the man had an air of confidence under stress—the sort that brought justice forward from killing chickens for their trespasses to a little sympathy under the law.

Yet he was no Penny Dreadful cutpurse—that was clear. Again, Sophie came to him in her beauty and he imagined leaving the pub with her. He had to speak to her, Max decided. He had been right in his vision out of perdition: love was the rope which he had to climb. This belief filled his soul, solidifying into a decision that must be acted out. And with that Max walked into the scorching heat of the Big Smoke's oven.

Chapter 23

Outside the air clung to him like grease and Max immediately began to sweat through his shirt and trousers. All around him people bustled, wandered, and stood—mostly stood—under the edifices of a previous opulence. Stakes, driven into the raw beating city, were the glass bastions of single-minded and all-devouring growth. Self-sufficient and isolated in their elevation above everyone else, but no man is an island and these islands were built by men. Unfettered by reality, but firmly fettered to the promise of better, they were struts to an invisible tent beginning to tear. Despite the depths of the darkness revealed, it was still there and under it the rest of the city lay like animals yoked in the zoo.

There were lions and zebras, bears and fish, all grouped together, all forced together—hierarchies crushed underfoot, and for what? The stringing of invisible and intangible tapestries for those who had forced themselves so far away from any breath of light that they were wide-eyed. What—no need to squint? Truly, this once great city had been lost to itself: so deep in its guts was its rattling tail that the only solution to its seismic trajectory was slicing it in two. This top to tail cut would lay bare all that had been, but looking at this defunct mess Max was dispirited and he wondered just how long the American Candy shops would stay there.

At home he was greeted by a text from Sophie, tentatively opening an alley of conversation. At first Max engaged gingerly with a couple of casual flourishes, but with her replies continuous so came lengthier responses. Sophie reciprocated and the conversation swelled. Max sensed a certain freshness coming from Sophie, something less playful and more elegant. In turn he gave way to himself and spilt through his self-reflecting charade. Their phone screens scurried upwards, away from the earnest interjections. As their thumbs hammered away at each's base they quickly dug up enough for a drink. Max was overwhelmed by her responsiveness and sat contorted on his sofa for an hour indulging in this back and forth—it was reminiscent of his teenage years. He hoped Sophie was in a similarly twisted state.

On and on they went and Max received a brief yet suggestive outline of her previous few months: a family occurrence, a job switch and a general rethinking of life. He ruefully thought of his own experience of this time and wondered quite how her "rethink" compared to his. Certainly, the tumult he'd passed through had gratifyingly deposited him on a high peak of transcendence, but the distance he felt from her ached. So too did the fact that as Max looked around at this great height he saw only further ascents, dressed with foreboding and obscuring clouds. Wherever Sophie was amongst these mountains, if even here, there was no zip wiring away to meet her. It was yet more climbs away, and only on the promise of a potential future meeting. Max ached even more as he thought of when they'd met, with its flowering ease and heated currents, and in the pits of his heart he longed to be dancing with her there.

They continued to talk, and Sophie felt a coalescence in the messages she received from Max. Where there had been a delightful and engaging outer and the hope of a warm and complex inner, there was now something new. He seemed to have overcome his dualism and she found more depth to the casual remarks ingratiating themselves to her now bubbling soul. She thought back to his features, and though she was a little rusty on their exact shape, colour and dimensionality flooded into the picture. Sophie looked at herself, along her arms, torso and legs, all capturing the tumult of the previous few months, and thought about how they'd been used and changed: a few specs of scab were left here and there, but what struck her was her newfound shapeliness and undulation. She clenched her shoulder blades and pulled her head back feeling the dramatic waves travelling downwards culminating in the bountiful arch of her lower back—a McQueen. Her body was aware of her experience in the forest and then in the copse; something had been found there, found inside of her.

Gaia seemed a flattening of what had been there—a compressing shorthand perhaps, but Sophie hadn't the words to describe it any further and so had to allow this crudity to loom over her mind like a singular icon. Somewhere between divined and divining she sat watching this spinning vision with its one piece flying around and around—or was she moving, chasing the hinted occupants of some eternal carousel?

She too worried about the Sophie Max would meet and how far away they might be from one another. Yet for her it was more of a difference of depth than breadth. In the wilderness, a concentricity contained her and all she might be, drawing towards herself everything that was hers, as much as it projected her outwards. There was a way forwards or backwards; the dichotomy stuck, and she sat in it, confused.

Bringing herself back to the sofa, or rather to its arm, Sophie too longed for the flirtatious freshness of their meeting with all its yearning simplicity. Very much the tactile type, she carefully ran a finger down her cheek, opening her mouth so as to swallow in the emerging valley. Sophie decided that whatever was to come should have to live up to the most ecstatic of her fantasies if it were to be worth interesting her. She had surfaced, needs and all, and she bathed in their warm spring, purring with delight at what must be in store. She was sure that Max was at the same place and so Sophie rubbed her thighs together in anticipation, longing for what pragmatism had so quickly cut mid-stem and reduced to a cold lack of personality. What Sophie wanted, she realised as all these feelings bubbled up and boiled back down into a dense heat in her groin, was a good fuck. At this she laughed a deep belly laugh, and almost spilt the bag of popcorn she'd been dextrously drawing from. All this to curl up in a brilliantly replete giggle.

Chapter 24

Max's joy bore him into the evening and he only roused himself for dinner. After pottering about the premises picking up this and that, stuffing and storing and pleasurably spinning his way through the mess, Max had some food and sat back down to wait. In the intervening time he scrolled up, scrolled down, flicked, and tapped—thumbing motion into the otherwise flat world in his palm. His angel Valentine came to mind, his swopping down at the last minute and offering a confounding clemency. The rozzers had been miffed again by the wielding of a gristly pastry and the pugnacious law.

Quite taken with this vignette, Max bobbed and nodded to himself like a toddler, vaingloriously muttering, "Barmy" this and "Barmy" that. Protected, the gift of Valentine's obfuscation drifted his crime into a distant memory. The tortuous affair and its humanising aftermath faded to a succession of, "You know what's" and developmental drivel. Max was far away, he thought, from the hunched figure who'd birthed *Ahriman* out of his palm pool; he looked back to it with the dull grin of someone who's forgotten they're running flat out. For now Max gorged and slurped in front of the blaring television with all the nauseating grandiosity of a king still living in the land of his mind's eye.

*

Sophie had settled in back at home and together the family fell into a comfortable rhythm. Alastair, Ed and John had all decided to work from home in the lead up to the funeral and had turned the dining room into a sort of shared office space. Alastair, ever the patrician, worked from files and so ended up ensconcing himself within a fort of the aforementioned after only a few days of the arrangement. The brothers busied themselves with their laptops and screens and, at least as far as Sophie was concerned, flogged themselves senselessly over nothing. Arthur was satisfied picking up work here and there and biding his time until he could figure out where he wanted to start.

Forestry was Arthur's passion. He'd spent his childhood trapping, climbing trees, and collecting plants and insects. However, although he had a bounding physicality, he could become a bit of a droopy dog on his darker days. Sophie had been noticing this more and more in his stolen moments when, like a long-standing pet, he would plod and pounce his way around the house. Sometimes Sophie's eyes followed his footsteps along the walls and ceiling as she sat reading in the dining room. Sophie also found herself playing with the "Feelings Stick," as the boys still insisted on calling it. The loss of momentum miffed her: life seemed to have been reduced to pawing through the dark. The unknown, Sophie decided, was more than the febrile war films she'd been raised on. Her adrenaline was spent and her cortisol was bankrupt; Sophie was adrift within herself.

However, this journey to the centre of the critic bored her quickly and her mind turned to life after the funeral. The prospect terrified her; the funeral was a watershed to hide behind, but being left in the lurch terrified her more. Although Sophie had accepted that nature would have to be a part of it;

"You can't be saved by some spirit of the forest," as she was calling it now, "And not accept it to be a part of your life to some degree," she thought to herself.

Beyond this Sophie was stumped so she ran through all the scum that was on the surface of her mind.

"Gardening…" she awkwardly pressed,

"Camper…," she wasn't even limiting herself to jobs apparently,

"Horticulturist…," not that she knew what that was. This measly platter she presented herself with had her longing fondly for the lifelessness of her previous career's slow decline.

All the while her mother's death hung like smoking drapes in some abandoned house, a cruel mockery of celebratory bunting, they leered down at Sophie and her family domineering retentively.

As Sophie came to, and on leaving her languor she saw the grindstone pressed heads of her male relatives buried in deaths of their choosing. On self-destructive missions to obliterate any of their softness, they drove themselves harder and harder against the screen, the file, the tool, forcing their matter into it and forcing dust to dust. Everything around Sophie seemed to be collapsing; the cosmos was noiselessly crashing together into the inevitable flashpoint of a crushing singularity. Here they would be forever moulded together into one grotesque form: a corrupted inky black lung pumping for itself with no one to see. Little flutters here and little flutters there but eventually, without purpose and usefulness, they would degrade down to perfect stillness, devoid of a past or a future—devoid of time.

"This can't be our fate," Sophie thought to herself as she returned to her experiences in the forests, wondering what else might become available to her on returning.

This twinge, once felt, fast became a beckoning, and amid the overlapping cycle she was pulled forth and back into the world she had so confidently left behind.

While Sophie had been emerging out of her cocoon, however, Arthur had continued his pacing around the house. The next morning he was out attending to various tasks around the property. Sophie heard the roar of his quad bike as he opened the throttle going up the ridges and hillocks behind the house. He was replanting a field, she knew, as well as clearing the wood behind the house of all the dead branches. These tasks would occupy him fully enough that he was able to spend most of the day out of that dreadful dining room. Arthur would only briefly return to the house for a shower before supper, or to pick something up. Sometimes he returned just to sit—that was how he spent most of the next week. This began to worry Sophie and she broached the subject to the rest of the family to no avail. Sophie longed for her mother—the fool's hope of a rose-tinted retrospective. The woman's cold removal had not been a mastery of the family's undercurrents, it was merely relegation to a decorative status.

Sophie saw that all the boys had literally buttoned themselves up since her mother's passing. Chequered shirts ranging from subtle to gaudy created, along with the work set up, a pseudo-pantomime in the house. Still, her mother played on Sophie's mind and she thought back to her childhood as the runt of the litter. She wondered what would have happened if she'd been born a boy? Who would she be now, at this moment, if she'd been like her brothers? The depths of this ocean of herself scared her quite deeply. In fact, as she thought about who she might have been she looked at her body and she realised that she saw it as a testament to what hadn't happened, rather than to what had. All the figures she'd seen, day in and day out for years innumerable, cascaded over her. They were a multiversal reappraisal of her eternal self. But these identikit options made her body feel even more alien. All the silicone weighting, more silicone and more sharpening; whatever could be torn more and more away from what was? But really? Was she to meet some matriarchal kraken in the depths of this icy ocean? Did her mother lurk below like the black heart of a crushing bog?

Bog bodies, they say, never die. They don't decompose and thousands of years; they are transfixed as if bound by Medusa. A gorgon, Sophie decided, was the ultimate matriarchal tyrant; it was the deliverer of impotence and the forcer of a chilling distance. Perhaps, Sophie wondered, the real difficulty for her was the gorgon's focus on men.

Chapter 25

Max was at a loose end: picking and folding had only taken him so far and he needed something new. Eventually, after much deliberation, Max opened his laptop to check on whatever might remain of *Ahriman*. Though he'd deleted everything there would surely be some fallout. His curiosity was rewarded and after only a brief scouring of various socials, Max had found a few titbits indicating what might have happened. *Ahriman* had seemingly become a byword for cataclysm, though he couldn't quite work out in reference to what. The word had begun to be used so ubiquitously that it'd been utterly dislocated from its original context—an empty epithet. So piercingly accurate, at one point, that the destruction associated with it was now put before its application. It had wiped itself from cyberspace—was meaning without context or was context without meaning? An archaeological anthropologist, he observed this self-swallowing ecosystem as if it were the half-digested fragments of the snake's tail deep within its intestines.

Eventually, after a lot of digging, Max found some useful evidence through posts and reposts, both narrowly following and preceding the deletion. The uproar from his devout fans was as horrifying as the elation of his detractors was sickening. Those in support had seen *Ahriman's* demise as the end of the future, the failure of the next step forward. His detractors, however, saw him as the final nail in the coffin of the modern world and his existence as an abomination. There was no middle-ground, ever a dichotomy, bleeding into itself, a clash of contexts and of extremes. More scrolling detailed the media's picking up of the story, mainstream publications, the news, of all things. Reluctant hacks and pundits manhandled his little game under the burning spotlight—a ridicule in itself, for both parties? Yet, melting under the glare of the nation's gaze, Max felt less and less answerable to their prodding assumptions. All was immaterial as *Ahriman* was proving in his returning to its world, the real world. Max looked up and all around his flat, realising that this, the world he had created for himself and grown as a seed from all the dense potential of his laptop, had become its own great shell; a thick knarled crust that deflected all their arrows.

*

This "world of a free agent" that he had so delicately tailored for himself, reminded him of his childhood. A fairly quiet upbringing, in Fulham—he really hadn't moved far he snorted to himself. And very little notable. It had been a long time since he'd spoken to his parents,

"They aren't even that far away," Max mused.

Yet he hadn't even phoned them in months. Their house and the home, the former before the latter, was incepted deep within the folds of his mind, a box inside a box inside a box, long since left to itself. But nothing that had happened made him feel any change needed to occur in their relationship.

He didn't dislike them, or like them, they simply weren't a part of his life. And they themselves were individuals to the last; hardly akin to nurturers of the familial brood. They had created themselves, created their life and created him. Then they had quietly looped their way back to the main road, leaving their diversion to course forward. Yet he was as full and bushy-tailed as ever,

"No runt here," Max thought to himself, "I am choice manifest" he said to himself.

The words hung in the air and Max grimaced a little at the bubble font they appeared in, a gauche immaturity, he thought to himself—they didn't settle in the way they used to. After everything that had happened recently, life seemed a little too possible; the spectre of *Ahriman* hung in his mind and Max shuddered, contracting his neck.

"Enough nostalgia," work was coming up.

Three jobs in quick succession, all two days long and all done in a week. He would need to get some kit together for them, but mercifully there was a van he'd be able to borrow off of a photographer friend to transport everything. All were outdoors and out of London allowing him to charge a lot extra for only a little legwork. Jobs like these were usually good money because more often than not they were for big, seasonal advertisements or at least some sort of promotion and they were always for the largest companies. The driving was a bore and the kit took time to collect, but it wasn't hard work and because no one knew he had been working significantly less than usual recently, they wouldn't blink at the increased rates.

Planning dealt with, what worried Max was that it would be the first time he'd been out of London since his mad dash out to the hinterlands with Matt's corpse. Steadying himself, he scratched his mind for the location of the drop-off point. All Max remembered, however, was that the location was,

"Past Reading... perhaps..." he nervously blinked to himself, "Perhaps it'll help that I don't know where it is, I don't have anything to tell the Police."

Dissatisfied with the puerile crudeness of this statement Max frantically rattled his brain trying to fire out some hint of detail, but none came. The absurdity: he had killed someone, dumped the body and now he couldn't remember where it was. The lurid comedy of this curdled his stomach and Max bent double only to gaze at the floor. What hubris had caused this he howled in his head. It was as though he had lost all the smarts that had allowed him to get away with it..!

Chapter 26

Sophie had been helping her dad with the funeral arrangements and together they neared the finishing touches.

"So, just to double-check, we are sure on burial over cremation," she asked.

"Yes," her father angrily retorted, "Of course, we've been over this how many times."

"I know," she replied, "But it's worth checking, everything gets pushed back if we change our minds."

"Yes, yes, very true, very true," somehow his daughter drew the fun out of logistics.

"So we've got us all doing some short speeches," she confirmed, "And the vicar has been sent the draft?"

"Yes, and Yes," replied her father, "She's very good, it'll all go well."

"Powell? Yes I suppose, I haven't seen her in years," Sophie said wistfully.

"You should meet her," Alastair urged, "Before the service I mean. She'll have something to say about everything, about the abruptness of it all. I really think you'd gain something from talking to her."

Sophie leant against her father's chair at the head of the table. They were alone in the dining room and the lights were turned low giving the walls a mottled effect.

"Maybe yes, maybe no. I'll see her anyway won't I?" Sophie cocked her head and raised an eyebrow at her father. This challenge was met with a fatherly squeeze from Alastair,

"I really think it'll be good for you," he said touchingly, "Everything has been so sudden for you, because of my decisions," he added awkwardly, "And I can see what you were trying to do with your feeling… stick…" the words fell out of his mouth with a natural resignation, "But you'll need more to… help you";

"Help us," Sophie interrupted, "It was for all of us and it was a first step."

"Yes…," Alastair hesitantly nodded, "But perhaps something akin to guidance rather than…. self-expression," he closed his gesturing hands with contented satisfaction.

"Perhaps," allowed Sophie, her resolve collapsed, "Yes you're right," she allowed.

"Right," her father declared with defining triumph, "I'll arrange for you two to meet!"

And so a couple of days later on a moody Wednesday morning, Sophie found herself walking down a thickly hedged country lane towards a distant spire.

*

A bright yellow tractor rounded the bend towards Sophie. Its driver was a relaxed and ruddy-faced neighbour who gave her a broad wave and gestured towards a break in the hedge. Obeying, Sophie nestled herself amongst the foliage and watched the mechanical mass pass her by, a gentle giant.

Behind it came a pokey little VW with mud flared behind each of its wheels and another ruddy-faced local with his gammoney hand rhythmically tapping an absent-minded beat on the outside of the driver's door. Again, the man gave a gentle wave to Sophie as she peeped out after the tractor, even bobbing his head with mock anger as she rolled her eyes and drew back in. Along he went, an old banger, assimilated into the surrounding world. Finally, however, came an enormous black four-by-four—its tinted windows and pristine finish declaimed it metropolitan. The G-wagon had a wide gait that filled all the available space between the overarching hedges, causing Sophie to shrink back into her nook and watch the behemoth pass in front of her. Inside was a couple with their two children: blonde and lithe, they wore blue Barbours and enjoyed their car's delicacy amongst themselves. The husband (the driver) gave Sophie a slow imperious glance that stopped right in front of her, barely registering her crumpled form. The dark mass heaved past the hedges, bending and breaking branches as they inexorably scraped along its glossy flank. The children were encased in a sort of faux cage with badly covered plastic bars. Each of their car seat cots was brightly coloured and had a mini mobile topping it, an afterthought thrust over them. Plastic bottles and child-rearing supports filled the rest of the back, climbing its sides like bricks building a wall. It was a truly objectionable sea of things and it crept past her helmed by its impatient captain, a boat navigating a busy dry dock.

It finally passed and Sophie stepped out to watch its slow retreat as the bushes enclosed and its obstinate bulk passed on. She thought she caught a glance from someone in the car but she couldn't be sure. The flash of a couple of whites and their boring pupils was enough to make her scowl and

Sophie dodged their gaze by glancing at the number plate which mockingly read "C H 3 1 T R K." Sophie turned around, disgusted, and looked up at the familiar spire, now cloaked by cloud—it was harmony.

She walked the rest of the way quickly; mercifully there was no oncoming traffic to delay her again and tacking up the wind, following the road left and right, she snaked closer and closer with every bend. Yet regardless of her beat Sophie could see the church in front of her a beacon in the near distance. Finally, she reached a wide break in the hedge that opened up to a view of the rolling hills behind it. The gravestones in the foreground formed a higgledy-piggledy bank, guiding her vision through to the church and its squat form settled comfortably in the landscape. Behind it was the beautiful tapestry of rural England, revealing itself before her in all its technicolour like an opening palm inviting her to hop on. Formed by man, for the land, the overlaid grid seemed a quilt under which the bed was kept clean and warm by tractors ploughing slowly across a scattering of the fields, fine combs tending to the stray hairs. Sophie was stuck by the calm before her and gingerly stepped past the framing walls and into the painting.

The path took her, root to trunk, to a low arch and old wooden door that opened into the dim interior within. Her eyes adjusted as she entered and she turned to see the sunlight streaming in through the stained glass above the door. She turned back and saw the grave slabs inscribed with the names and dates of dead saints buried underneath the church. As she did so the squat figure of Vicar Powell entered the nave and shot a kindly hello at Sophie's twisted figure. Sophie decided that the Vicar must have been in her late fifties or sixties. The bob she wore was cut below the ears and a pair of spindly glasses were balanced on the bridge of her nose. She had a timely grace that accompanied her through the church.

"Sophie, it's so lovely to see you, how are you?" the vicar breathed.

This question drifted towards Sophie and somehow wrong-footed her; all she was able to give in reply was a vague,

"Uhuh."

Vicar Powell took her hand and led her towards the first pew on the right. Together the pair sat in silence for a few seconds as both gazed up at the cross in front of them.

Above them was a scrawny figure whose ribs popped out and whose torso had been punctured at least twenty times. Along with that of the stigmata, the blood from his wounds streamed down his xylophonic frame and stained his translucent skin an ugly vermillion. His knees were knocked and forced together as if he were already a corpse while his eyes were wide and downcast, betraying the last vestiges of a life filling his fleshless vessel. Sophie had, of course, seen crosses like this before at school but sitting underneath one now put her under the full weight of its compelling gaze.

Together they sat under this horror, saying nothing, until Vicar Powell eventually broke the silence with another vast open question,

"So, how are you doing?"

It was this awful sincerity that she found so hard, Sophie decided. Since she had found out about her mother's death and been forced to deal with the failures of her family, Sophie had been working under the bounds of a yearning sincerity and it was exhausting. "To wake up each and every day and honestly bring all her fullest self to the forefront of her experience was extraordinarily draining," the voice said. It was all, after all, the exact inverse of the conscious withdrawal of herself from her life which had armoured her through her time at the V&A. While the former seemed an ever pouring of herself into the bottomless receptacle of life, the latter seemed a never-ending emotional retrenchment that kept Sophie scratching the bottom of her unsatiated inner. And what good were either of these extremes if they yielded the same life-sapping results? All this drove up within her like the tide caught in a reservoir and, turning to look at Vicar Powell, Sophie's inner turmoil spilt out into her cheek's capillaries. The Vicar put a comforting palm on Sophie's now balled fists, embracing them with a cooling touch;

"Loss is hard," she murmured, "Especially so when it's so unexpected."

The inanity of these statements enraged Sophie and she stood up, turned to Vicar Powell, and shouted,

"Easy for you to say—your life must be as devoid of spontaneity as it is of a personal fucking touch!"

Vicar Powell was stunned, but waited for Sophie to continue her tirade. Sophie spluttered on as the world span with her,

"What the fuck would you know about something like this, huh? I've been sent here to what, get some fucking ecumenical counsel? What the fuck am I meant to do with that, fucking flagellate myself with a fucking flense?"

"Golly, you know a few words beginning with 'F' don't you? Anything else I should know?" Vicar Powell fired back under a raised eyebrow. The sarcasm of this retort knocked Sophie off balance and her vehement spittle turned to a bumbling dribble. The Vicar continued, "My child, unfortunately covering yourself with fury won't help you deal with the death of your mother, unfortunately nor do I have a magic bullet."

Her face now restored a little Sophie replied, "Well obviously," and with nihilistic dejection, "I know that."

"Well if you know that then why are you here, and why are you angry if what's happening is what you expected?"

This froze the conversation and defanged Sophie enough for Vicar Powell to continue unhindered.

"You've come because your father thought talking to me would help you deal with the emotions you have surrounding your mother's tragic passing. You knew what you were coming for and despite the layers of this sacred place enthralling you, as they do I, I am simply another human who can offer advice. What you think you're looking for is here, but it's the wrong thing to be looking for and that's why you're angry. God has given me everything I have: my life, my loves; my experiences, and now this place. You aren't looking for me, you're looking for God, and I think that some part of you knows this."

"Here ends the first verse," Sophie thought to herself. "I'm not looking for God, I have God— a God at least," Sophie replied.

"Oh do you?" Vicar Powell said with slight affection and another raised eyebrow, "Why not go to this God then, instead of coming to me?"

"I suppose because I don't know how to get to my God, it comes to me. Or rather, it brought me to it and does so when it wants me, or rather when I need it."

"It sounds like you have a rather one-sided relationship with this god then," Vicar Powell said softly.

"Maybe, I'm not so sure," Sophie pressed, "It doesn't feel one-sided, it feels there's something of it inside me, or at least something inside me that's equal to it."

"God is inside all of us," Vicar Powell said, squaring herself and bringing her hands on top of one another in a sermonic stance.

"No I don't mean it like that," Sophie continued, "it's not a part of it inside me, they are equal." At this Vicar Powell took a beat and seemed to be weighing potential replies in her gaze; each eye had an option hanging heavily within, with neither having the aplomb to raise the other. She steadied herself with a palm planted on either side of her and rose up with an air of reticence unnatural to her.

"Sophie," she began slowly, "Is this an attempt at theological discourse or are you perhaps digging into a part of your brain best left to itself?"

"And is blasphemy still a crime?" Sophie shrugged back in exasperation, "My mother's died!"

Vicar Powell mentally chided Sophie for such childish impertinence, it arose at every challenge Vicar Powell made to her pseudo-spiritual drivel. This sort of "oh God in me, my God" always struck her as far too narcissistic a beginning point for any meaningful connection with God. Yet it seemed it was ever more common these days, given what she gleaned from fellow clergy and an attention to the news. It was no surprise that Sophie's coming was the first of its kind in a long time, Vicar Powell thought. Where did discussions like these fit into the world as it was now? It didn't shake her faith but it did make her wonder how best she could be of use as a Vicar. People like Sophie, she mused, seemed to believe themselves the Alpha and the Omega and that everything in between was a perfectly mapped maze that only needed travelling through. The world of these people must be so flat, the Vicar thought, so reduced that the most human behaviours must be alien to their well corralled minds. This saddened Vicar Powell and she thought about her choice to stand firm and wait for the would-be congregation to come, rather than leave and pursue a more active approach. What the latter option might entail was a mystery in itself and, as she glanced up at the crucifix behind Sophie, she was reminded of how Christ progressed on his mission. It was nothing less than his steady faith in God that had won the day and the changes iterated by his father's warm uninterrupted gaze.

"Sophie, why don't you come to a service? Often, I find that more is revealed when I commit myself to the rituals of worship. And I enjoy the camaraderie," the Vicar added with a kindly nod of her head."

"Boilerplate," Sophie thought to herself, "As much a contract as any other I've signed." This parallel's absurdity struck her but, as she looked at the placid face of Vicar Powell, Sophie realised the clergywoman was, for good or ill, the embodiment of yet another impersonal devotion.

The whispers of the forest spoke to her whipping through the church. This was enough for her to shake her head and politely decline Vicar Powell's offer. What she needed, Sophie decided, it had to be her own to find and create for herself.

Vicar Powell sensed this and silently hoped to herself that it would be brief and deep rather than long and shallow.

"People wander barefoot for miles expecting to find a river without realising the spring beneath," the vicar thought to herself.

Sophie saw something she thought to be resignation in Vicar Powell's intelligent eyes and remarked to herself on the experiential helplessness of each in terms of the other.

"Truly, only something larger than ourselves can bind us together," Sophie thought.

At this she looked up at the church's roof and saw the mass of cobwebs and rotting wood for the first time. The lustre was lost and Sophie found herself standing in the shell of a long-dead animal—gasping and parched in its calcification.

Chapter 27

Once again Max was sitting in the interrogation room, but this time Valentine was next to him. They sat in silence, apart from Valentine's heavy breathing which seemed to brew like steam in the back of his mouth. The room was warm and Valentine dabbed the sweat on his forehead with tissues he'd taken from the café they'd met in earlier. A few days ago Valentine had rung to explain that Officers N'kimbo and Richardson had scheduled another interview today, the Thursday, and that they were to go along. Valentine had informed him that they would have to reform their approach after the last interview and that he'd brief Max on their plan of attack over a coffee before it. The technicalities had been lost on Max, but the thrust of it was that whatever the two officers brought to the table Valentine would force the conversation back to something that drove a wedge between them. In effect this meant anything that would baffle N'kimbo's greenhorn understanding of police work or anything that would enrage Richardson's working-class roots. Again, the strategy's utter divorce from the facts of the case confused Max greatly, but he was still unwilling to enter into that particular conversation and so took Valentine's word that it was the right way to go. It seemed the opposite of justice to Max, but if it worked he was free and off the hook, and then what? He'd be able to see Sophie tomorrow evening, whom he'd been desperately looking forward to seeing since they arranged a drink, without any of this hanging over him. Max thanked God, in a sense, that the meeting was today as he was seeing her tomorrow night. A good outcome here would clear all of this unpleasantness away and they'd just be kids out for a drink. A bad one wasn't worth thinking about and so he simply put his trust in Valentine and hoped for the best.

Eventually, after the pair had been left to sweat in the empty interrogation room for a good hour, the air conditioning burst into life just as the two officers came in through the door. N'kimbo entered first but his stern expression gave way to the more foreboding knitted eyebrows and dark grimace of Richardson behind him. The officers' height difference was exacerbated from Max and Valentine's sitting position and the shorter stubbier figure of Richardson looked ever so slightly absurd behind the taller and slimmer N'kimbo. The latter's finely formed features and six-foot-something height were brilliantly illuminated by the white halogens not so far above. In this light he looked somewhat cybernetic especially against the comparatively ectopic Richardson, as if his skin were made of carbon fibre. N'kimbo was in the left-hand chair opposite Max, while Richardson, the bulldog, took the right one opposite Valentine. A mutual glint was visible in each of the pair's eyes at the professional pleasure of seeing one another again.

Max felt like a pawn and endeavoured to frame the interview in terms favourable to him, so presumed to begin,

"Well, hello officers, so good to see you again."

But before he could continue with what would have no doubt been an attempt at sincerity worthy of Hugh Grant, Valentine grabbed hold of the reigns and muscled Max out of the driving seat,

"Right officers, where did we get to last time? You were pushing and prodding my client without any evidence and without me to show you the error in your ways. I've dealt with the latter by turning up, now why don't you deal with the former by presenting some evidence for an actual case?"

N'kimbo's nose flared and he opened his mouth to begin but Valentine's eyes hadn't left Richardson and it was the stubby officer who began the offensive,

"Now Mr Valentine there's no need to be like that," the officer's jocular tone raised N'kimbo's eyebrows while igniting a fire in Valentine, "We understand there was a bit of drama in our last meeting but we only meant to appeal to Max's generosity," his cockeyed gaze and its accompanying confidence turned towards Max, sickening as it went, "Now Max you don't want to be here, and no doubt Mr Valentine here has told you he's going to help you not to come back, but there are certain processes we need to go through regardless."

Richardson's cockney swing cleared Valentine's natural fog and exposed the barebones foundations of Scotland Yard's handbook. Severely unsettled, Max's powerlessness deepened under the yoke of these two apparent giants of legal cat and mouse. There was so much drawing of battlelines Max thought to himself; it was frame against frame and he looked to Valentine to captain him through it. Richardson continued,

"As Mr Valentine kindly established we don't have much to go on. But we do have hours and hours of tape from all over London from that night," his mouth curled into a smirk,

"And Max this stuff takes days and days to go through, weeks really," he pushed himself away from the table and leaned back, "It takes ages but eventually we do get through it," his voice boomed with an unpleasantly assured tone, "And when we do we find snippets of information here and there, and once we've got them all together," he drew this pooling in the air, "We begin assembling them to create a picture of what the city already knows. And I tell you every time I've done this, and there have been a few," he gave a Max a wink, "I've come to find I already know what the city knows," and he finished, "Then we arrest the culprit." Max was chilled to the bone.

N'kimbo had the sense not to come in and simply sat next to his subordinate in a cool silence observing Max's now washed-out, features. Even Valentine had to take a beat and gather himself after this statement of process; Richardson had taken control of the room.

It was as if the cogs of a long-since-turned-off machine were finally warming back up again and their rhythmic click could be heard from building to building. The behemoth that was the exactitude of the Great British justice system approached, casting its long shadow ahead. It seemed undeniable to Max. However, behind it lay its spills and leaks and Valentine knew that if they could resist the dizzying sight of precedent piled on precedent, they could skirt around and nibble at the exposed parts of its accumulated power. Together they were bottom-feeding barnacles that, once attached, corroded away their purchase to allow them to fall back into the weight of their host, never to be seen again. This was Valentine's plan in a nutshell, Max realised, to feint the weight of the Police beside them and avoid guilt by letting overburdened necessity force their pursuers onwards. It was an overworked juggernaut that was reactive in its dysfunction and practical in its actions. This was what N'kimbo was unprepared for, and indeed what Richardson had been born for. The rules of the real world didn't exist in flatulent dystopias like this and N'kimbo's theorising was no match for a sixth-sense-smooth-operator like Richardson. The stubby hairball was a relic, in that anyone who knew anything was desperate to preserve him. The finickers and philanders may look down at him, with his appreciation of everything brown and edible and his white bread attitude to life, but the reality was that they were no match for his doggedness in the fight for what was right.

Now under the cosh and very much the wiser, Valentine shuffled in his seat, tapped his papers into step, and exhaled slowly through his nose.

"But Officer Richardson," he began smoothly accompanied by a languid pull of his beard, "No one here would doubt your…," he paused for emphasis and waved his hands with an almost effusing quality "Affinity with the city," he came back down to earth, "Nor would anyone doubt your dedication to the job but you're hardly painting a picture that my client can finish off for you," he shot a leading glance at N'kimbo in the hope he'd see this as his opportunity to rein in his deputy, "I can't stop the wheels of justice and I certainly don't plan to try," another increasingly pointed look at N'kimbo, "But you're asking me to defend my client against shadows in the night," and at this Valentine opened his palms to the heavens with a deep shrug.

N'kimbo was willing to stay in the backseat and waited patiently for Richardson to respond. His first case in London was significantly more dramatic than expected. He thought about his conversation with Richardson in the car after their visit to Max's flat and the undercurrents of his subordinate's contribution.

"I know you're not one of them!"

It rang in his ears and cracked open to reveal a wholly different intention. N'kimbo thought back to his first post, in beautiful Buckinghamshire, where he'd cut his teeth. In a strange way he had fitted in as a man with a discernible reason for being there. Policing had as much structure there as the cottages he'd knocked politely on the doors of, while here, now promoted, N'kimbo felt like a loose bit of seaweed; victim to the movements of currents far too large and intangible for him to understand.

The rapport between Richardson and Mr Valentine was palpable, and no doubt the consequence of the common law they shared like bickering neighbours. N'kimbo wondered what it must be like for someone like Richardson in this day and age; as far as N'kimbo knew Richardson had lived in East London his entire life, and apart from his 'boy done good' edge that was it. It must be strange now that the 'Real Villains' had all but disappeared and been replaced by a completely different lot whose foreign heritages were alien to him. Crime had changed, London had changed; success had changed, everything had changed, and it had done so from the top leaving those like Richardson without a place.

"Max," Richardson began again, "These things take time but we will get to the bottom of what happened to your friend. There will be a lot more of these," he gestured to the room, "And more rounds of the same for your friends. So I highly suggest you cooperate for your own sake and theirs," he paused to let his words sink in,

"What do you know about Matthew's death?"

"I really don't know anything," Max stammered.

As the last syllable leaving his lips Valentine came back in, forcing the conversation back to Richardson. The two returned to the fray and once again N'kimbo and Max were left facing each other, each a secondary part to the main show. Both were utterly out of their depth and as they looked blankly at each other they saw that, despite their differences, they had more in common than their warring partners. N'kimbo certainly didn't pity Max; he was still of the opinion that he'd killed Matt but he could sense something in the him that indicated a linguistic similarity. Max felt a familiarity with his senior arresting officer for much the same reasons. There was something so very functional about the both of them. They were citizens of everywhere and citizens of nowhere and their lack of identity or ideology were versions of the same. They had been born out of an attempt to flatten the world, to export and absolve and to tame nature. Like rubber ducks they were meant to float on the calmed surface of this 'world water feature'. Its unified ugliness brought together the lowest common denominator in qualities with the highest percentage of specialization. They were the ever sharpening of the most basic tools—a hammer and sickle. Theirs was a gilding of the necessary in lieu of the flourishing of the bountiful and as they looked at each other over the grey desk they wondered what funny little costumes each would next be wearing. No doubt they'd have moved on to bigger and better things, mentally they already had, while their champions would still be fighting a battle as old as time.

"Will he let me go?" Max thought to himself,

"Will he let me stay?" N'kimbo thought the same.

It wasn't chess they were playing, but draughts. Black and white weren't in opposition—it was black and red, but they were on the same side regardless. And this was where they now saw each other—each besides their representative. They were not two sides of the same coin but rather one amorphous metallic blob.

Chapter 28

The firing had ceased and now Valentine and Richardson stood amongst the glowing embers of the fray. But there would be another meeting, that was a definite. Richardson was determined to coax Max into betraying himself and he could see that Valentine was running out of moves. Valentine, for his part, was convinced that N'kimbo could be enticed to take the investigation in another direction if Valentine's pressure on Richardson caused the junior to show too much of himself. If pushed hard enough, Valentine's cockney constable would be forced to outrank N'kimbo entirely. And should the investigation take this direction that would be enough to halt proceedings. However, Richardson had seen deeper into Max and was now fully convinced that the boy was both guilty and enough of a drip that he'd topple with one well-placed blow. One piece of circumstantial evidence and a confession would ensue.

*

Despite appearances Richardson was no Machiavelli. His childhood had been stark: his cradle was in the flats and his lullabies were the throng of violence, but he looked back at it fondly in so much as it had given him the necessary materials and momentum to make a firm choice about who he wanted to be. There had been violence in his youth, but it had been outside the home and, guided by a quiet assuredness and a little luck, Richardson had managed to pick his way through it largely unscathed. This had allowed him to enter the working world unjaded and had gained him speedy success—at least in part for simply being uncorrupted. But it was his streetwise doggedness that had given him a lasting career in the force, and this was what he now wielded in front of Max with frightening skill. Unfortunately that which had gifted Richardson his rise had also caused a plateau. He had decided to work in all the major departments before making the jump to a senior desk-jockeying position as he felt a full aggregation of all possible practical knowledge to be a moral imperative for a 'pencil pusher'. However, this more holistic attitude to policing had delayed that crucial thirty-something career jump long enough that it was pushed to the turn of the millennium and to the beginning of the disillusionment that had plagued the public services ever since. New Labour's abandoning of the working class had pained Richardson deeply and he felt wrenched from the institution he had planned on devoting his entire career to. Furthermore, the incompetence and corruption that had been virtually encouraged by this disregard had disadvantaged those of his moral persuasion. Taken together these two factors had all but stalled his career leaving him in a limbo where someone like Officer N'kimbo could find him.

The pseudo-mentoring of his, apparently senior, officer had infuriated Richardson both as a task itself and as a capsule example of the nature of the modern force. Officer

N'kimbo was utterly unlike any of the blacks he'd ever met. There had been plenty on the estate where he'd grown up, and everyone had managed to become friends. He wasn't surprised that Officer N'kimbo hadn't been brought up with the 'principles' he had. He was posh—that was inevitable. It was his aloofness that Richardson hated.

For Richardson growing up, racial differences had been something to be actively moved past in the day-to-day but celebrated on the special occasions. Officer N'kimbo, however, seemed to deny their very existence. The man just wouldn't give that part of himself into their conversations, he wouldn't play the game of differences. Richardson had initially thought this was the case because Officer N'kimbo didn't understand that he, Richardson, didn't think of them as anything more than an inconsequence. However, he had lately come to realise that his superior simply refused to give any of himself to someone like Officer Richardson. This was clear and distinct classism in Richardson's opinion, and he had learnt long ago in the flats not to allow himself to be a victim of it. But there was nothing to be done when Officer N'kimbo became his senior. It had only become worse after that because, despite his education, Officer N'kimbo didn't have any loyalty to those below him and so he rejected all but what he felt were the truly necessary aspects of the force. The deal that Richardson felt he had been born into had ceased to exist. Worse still it had happened under a Blairite government only to be buried even deeper under the subsequent Conservatives. Richardson hated the Tories with an inherited passion, but even he knew on some level that all the carnage they had overseen had been the worsening of that began by Labour, and this stung worse than everything. The principles of his youth, those adages of practicality, had been torn apart from above. His, and those from his childhood's, efforts to dignify themselves and to make themselves morally upwardly mobile had been ridiculed by the power keepers at the top.

Lastly, and most strangely for Richardson, he didn't even recognise his own estate. It had transformed into genuine squalor, rid of any notion of respect. Most confusingly of all there were genuine ethnic issues, as far as he could see, which couldn't be addressed by him of all people or by people like Officer N'kimbo! The ridiculousness of this state of affairs sometimes choked him with anger, and when he ventured to the pub with the old boys he found himself needing to quench his thirst with increasingly large amounts of lager. This had led to the beard and the podge which only lowered himself in his eyes. All he saw now was this link between N'kimbo, a man quite contentedly and by default, estranged from his upbringing and Richardson's dislocation from his own. It was infuriating. His partner's tall elegance apparently wasn't enough for him to be teased as a giraffe, but it was enough for him to swan through all the shit he caused. This man, a shade in Richardson's world of characters, was antithetical to life itself.

Next to Richardson's ball of tension Officer N'kimbo was placid, and he was content to let his subordinate wind himself up for a while. Eventually, however, the officer found himself breaking the silence, a little too early perhaps, with a light cough into his delicately enclosed fingers.

"Mr Valentine," he began, "We've made our position clear and as far as I can see there's very little for you to argue with," he turned to Max, "Max, it's a simple question: what do you know about Matt's disappearance? My colleague, I think, has explained it in clear enough fashion." He eyed Richardson guardedly, "There are lengths that will be gone to regardless of your cooperation. We've simply asked you here to expedite an investigation in process … So, do you have anything to say?"

Max looked from N'kimbo to Richardson and back. The commanding officer's impassiveness had given way to a stern expression by the time his gaze had returned. He collected himself and pressed his clammy palms into the smooth linen of his light trousers.

"Officers I really don't have anything to tell you," he stammered out, "You keep calling these meetings but I really have nothing useful to say. I'm scared," he confessed, "I turn up and you have nothing to accuse me of. I have nothing to say and I need a lawyer to represent me for something I don't even know if I've apparently done. It's mad and I just want everything to stop. Truly I have nothing to tell you." Max's gripping hands relaxed into soft caressing palms sitting atop his now steady thighs. Time was up.

Valentine went through some closing statements but they were ultimately superfluous and soon the pair were walking quickly through the warrens below Charing Cross Police Station. They strode through their cold grey surroundings in silence and it wasn't until they were outside that Valentine addressed Max.

"Ball's in their half Max. You did well, don't worry too much."

Chapter 29

Back in his flat the evening was long and lonely. Max knew that despite his efforts the beginning of his and Sophie's connexion would have to take place in the shadow of this great henge. That monument to everything that he was trying to convince himself, as much as everyone else, was irrelevant to his being.

*

When Saturday evening finally came around Max and Sophie made their respective ways to Soho. Sophie had come back to London that afternoon, dropping her things off at a friend's, and since her meeting with Vicar Powell on Wednesday she had done very little. The family had had supper together each night as usual but little was said about the funeral. Alastair was disappointed by the report he'd received from Vicar Powell, whose curt summary went as follows,

"She's delusional and needs something to do."

Alastair had hoped Vicar Powell would have been able to instil a little calmness in his daughter whose preoccupation worried him somewhat, but the clergywoman seemed to have taken offence at something Sophie had said. Alastair himself was hardly practising, he wouldn't be expecting an apology from the liturgy. He was more worried about any issues between the Vicar and the family that might spill over into the funeral.

"Sophie, dear Sophie," he wondered to himself, "What do I have to do?"

In London, however, Sophie was in a buoyant mood now that she was finally meeting Max properly; and eager, if anything, to spend time with someone who didn't know what had happened to her mother. The night was cool, she was dressed lightly as she walked east towards Piccadilly and caught the final flecks of summer. To Sophie's left were all the rat runs filled with restaurants and behind her were the hotels between Green Park and Hype Park Corner. In front of her was an even more gaudy prospect; the walk between Piccadilly Circus and Leicester Square.

"Such a painful walk," Sophie had thought to herself on the previous leg of her journey. Passé opulence devoid of any elegance let alone a sense of place. It was the demesne of the haves and haves and haves and resembled a global warehouse of golden spare parts: aesthetically, spiritually and formally bankrupt—so much a reflection of so little that one had to pinch oneself to remind one that some such place could even exist. Sophie had realised that this hodge podge, with its accompanying camel coats wasn't to her taste and she shook a little at this rejection of her by her once Elysian London. Yet, as she neared Eros she raised her head to let the neon dance across her face and all was cleared away, smoothing her high cheekbones. Sophie slowed to feel the wash of the city take her up and bundle her in. Her eyes fell and for the first time in months she saw Max's slouching figure in front of her.

Their eyes met, awakening from their estranged slumber, and they hurried towards each other. They were finally able to see each other as clearly as they had on that night months ago. Before anything could be said, however, they simply gazed at one another beholding what they saw. Each could feel the other's change as much as they could feel their own, yet familiarity took a step forward just as the unknown stepped back. Finally dimensional, the paper took the ink, masked now, once and forever, finally centred in this paradox they were truly together.

For Sophie, Max's kindly crooked smile and stark features stood before her like safehavens on an unfilled map. But what swirled below she wasn't familiar with. So much given, Sophie could see, what now remained? In Sophie, however, Max saw the warm green eyes that sent him back to when they had first landed on his agape expression. It was the coquettishness that had disappeared, replaced by a fullness foreign to his eye. Whether she was an agrarian English rose or a cosmopolitan temptress, Max decided they needed to start getting to know each other again.

"Hi…," he began.

Conversation tumbled out quickly and effortlessly as they strolled north into Soho, as if to pass straight through this hive of activity, but then they turned east towards Leicester Square, and embraced it all over again. In this manner they lapped up the atmosphere, rounding on themselves over and over again until they found a bar. Inside they nestled themselves in a booth, deep in the rear, with a view out onto to the light-dappled street. A drizzle had begun, no doubt the beginning of the humidity breaking under its own weight, turning the glass exterior wall into a wash of colour that illuminated the dingy bar. Their drinks came and they sat opposite one another running their fingers up and down the cold moist glass.

Max with his meltwater rawness and Sophie with her blooming fullness simply looked at one another, waiting for one of them to open the floodgates.

"I'm sorry we haven't got together sooner, it's been a strange few months for me," Max began—a timorous pawn.

"I understand. It's been a difficult few months for me too."

"The Police…," Max began, "I've had to have a few interviews with them and it's been quite draining if I'm honest. Nothing's come of it, of course, and I'm not actually accused of anything, but it's unpleasant nonetheless."

"I can only imagine," Sophie's eyes deepened and she gave him a caring smile.

"What about you, how have you been keeping then?" Max asked with a boyish ruefulness.

"Not amazingly" and changing her mind, "My mother's passed … The funeral is in a week's time."

"My God"! "I'm so sorry, that's awful!" Max gave her a pitying grimace and her hand an affectionate squeeze. The conversation took a beat. The transparency—why did they communicate this way?

And yet for the first hour or so the conversation continued in this fashion. Each pawed at the ball, nudging it towards the other without the gumption to grab it. But, slowly, as they unwadded from their emotional crisping, the drinks flowed and something akin to laughter began to echo. Sophie explained she'd quit her job and talked about all the tiny little things she wasn't going to miss. Max giggled as he derided the vapidity of the actors he worked with and the utter debasement of the industry pros who handled them. It was all fucked, they agreed: this, that, and everything else.

They didn't have the energy to reveal any more of the crosses they had to bear; these were behind them, shrouded by the dark of everything that existed outside of the warm glow of their booth. Heavily cowled, each retreated further and further away from their respective hosts, unwelcome as the evening jollied along.

*

The rain had begun to abate and outside lay the most beautiful world; a freshly cleaned London with all its darkling crags sat just outside, waiting to be enjoyed by the delighting couple. And as their phones blinked to midnight they got their things together and left hand in hand. Outside their arms slinked around one another, curling into one another's rubbing bodies.. Their legs clattered, they ground together, tripping one another up as they turned further in towards each other.

Finally, they came to a halt in the centre of a crossroads with the moon sitting above them illuminating them under its pale gaze. Sophie looked up at Max with an expectant glee and Max looked down at her with a desiring determination. And, after months of waiting, they kissed.

Chapter 30

The door gave way behind her back as Max stepped through the frame, carrying Sophie into her temporary accommodation. Inside she leaned back and thrust her hips hard into his stomach giving him a view of wicked seduction and hiking herself further and further up on top of him. Much to her pleasure, Sophie rubbed herself up and down his stomach as they kissed while Max slowly walked them into the kitchen. There he put her down and Sophie stepped backwards delicately until she was pressed up against the wall, thrusting her chest forward. Max stood in the centre of the kitchen and looked at her, the object of his desires, his redemption, and breathed deeply to steady himself. She was now a beckoning vision melting all else away—a product of the previous few months. Sophie cocked her head to one side, raised an eyebrow, and opened her mouth ever so slightly in expectance. The sight was so besotting, in fact, that the thought occurred to Max to crawl to her instead and begin the kissing from below.

Somehow they made it to the staircase and Max drove upwards as Sophie kissed and licked his neck until he'd carried her into the room and thrown her onto the bed. For hours they were pressed together, grabbing and squeezing, extracting every last drop from one another. It had been so long. There was no patience for waiting and they gave each other everything they had, all that they had been holding for those long months apart.

*

Later they splayed across one another, drenched in sweat with an ashtray between them. The duvet was long gone and the floor-to-ceiling windows were wide open, letting in a much-needed cool breeze. Max lay on his back with a pillow squashed under his head while Sophie's head rested on his chest, her limbs wrapped tightly around him. Her beautiful eyes looked up at him with flushed cheeks and a gleaming satisfaction, almost breaking him open. All Max's recent anguish welled up under his eyes, straining he desperately retrenched under gasping breaths, apparently overwhelmed by the intimate passion. She was his deliverance, he decided, she did not know it, of course, but she gave him everything he needed to know of what it was to be him. It was she was who made the journey worth ending, she was what made home and he could feel the silken thread that bound him to her beckoning fingers.

They kissed.

Sophie looked up at his dark kindly eyes, telling her enough but holding back still more. His angular features had softened and the world behind them was begging to surface. She ran her fingertips along his chin, around his lips, and over his nose and then eyebrows, tilling the ground for a sprouting rebirth.

They talked in slow low voices, taking turns to usher the world along past them. The room's white walls went from black to grey as the night deepened into those forgotten hours between plans and waking. The temperature cooled and they drew each other closer, hugging tightly lest they must release themselves from their cocoon.

Could this sustain them for long? Could it last the night?

They lay together, no doubt scared to part, in vain hopes of a possible future, waiting, biding their time, until maybe it was their turn to become what lay outside the bedroom door. Neither was ready to face either what that might be or what their fraternising finally was—they were content to skim the liminality. But the day would come calling and as their nuzzling slowed and their lips relaxed their grips softened and their bodies fell deeper and deeper into an eventual sleep.

As the night passed both dreamt. Max saw his desert before him, torn asunder by rivers under the starlit sky, while Sophie was brought back into the great oak she had found sanctuary in on that terrible day. The shifting sands were stilled and the river's course was being calmly broken by the silent foaming of its processional white water. Meanwhile, the light striking the oak became the night sky and in Sophie, in her embryonic form, a new light grew snuggled safely in her cupping stomach.

If anyone were to have watched them that evening they would have seen the pair pawing at each other and their squiggling backwards and forwards. Together and apart. They played like this all night, their dreams competed for dominance in the subconscious world until they eventually turned away from one another, each pressing their backs against the other's. It was like this that they slept the night and although they clung to themselves in that cool room, they stayed pressed together warming one another. It was a powerful image that they formed and any observer would have stood a while, morosely even, before stealing their peace. This was no stay of execution, however, the hand only rests, it never leaves, but it was a sight.

Chapter 31

Sophie's friend had kindly let her stay the night but would apparently be back late morning. Neither fancied rummaging around someone else' fridge for breakfast materials, and so, after a quick shower, they dressed and headed out to a nearby café. The pair passed through a London wincing under the last dregs of summer. It was August, the humidity was cutting a little each day now and slowly the city's overwhelming glare was ratcheting down to a moodier middling autumn. The parks were unseasonably covered by leaves—the summers had been confused of late. Everything spoke to flux, something akin to an inevitable entropy.

It was becoming clearer to Sophie that Max's visitation to the Police was an ongoing process. His newfound fullness of character revealed how preoccupied with it he was, and it forced her to wonder why the authorities sustained their interest. Max, for his part, saw the stillness plying Sophie that subdued the turmoil induced by her mother's death and felt alienated by this prescient placidity. More and more their minds began to wander, each sneaking increasing side-eyes at the shops and passing cars; striding further and wishing for the certainty that unrolled behind them and lead back to their night's bed. Despite this, each knew their shared path forward, though it fragmented in front of them, only stood a change of salvaging them if they pressed on regardless. Doom, gloom, and strife shrouded Max's vision while dejected apathy descended on Sophie's.

Yet as they rounded the corner to the café of choice their spirits were lifted by a child dancing outside on the pavement under the watchful eye of his parents. He pranced from side to side like a bounding star, arms and legs outstretched through the hoop neck onesie he'd managed drag over his head like a cowl. In his left hand, he held a toy fire truck with an adjustable ladder, and in his right a red Mini with the Union Jack printed on its white top. The child, apparently unaware he had the entire café as an audience was hopping from one leg to the other, giggling as he did so. The parents had his younger sister, a baby, sitting on their table safely occupied with a rattle and a bib, each kept an eye arrested on a child.

The sight stopped the lovers in their tracks as they watched this child play. Possibilities of emotions shot through each of them and eventually turned them towards one another, holding the gaze. Meanwhile, the child had yanked his top down, turned around to his parents, and yelped with glee as he displayed his toys to their nodding faces. Now backstage to the performance Max and Sophie returned to the child and felt a settling overcome them.

Beckoned back to his parents, the child received cooing waves and looks of delight as he toddled across the veranda, regenerating as he went. For Max, a sense of perspective descended over him and he saw his lifeline broaden before his eyes. For Sophie, a sense of wholeness filled her, extinguishing the divesting fragmentation that had inhabited her. The café scene, on its picturesque stage, reminded Max he might once have appreciated how Sophie fitted in to his world, yet now he rejoiced at his realisation that she already had.

A posteriori to a priori, a reframing complete, rendering him amnesiac to everything pre-singularity, everything in utero. Sophie turned to face Max and, greeted by his bedazzlement, took his outstretched arm and allowed herself to be turned back around. Affronted, she found herself growing into this gifting gesture, her own hand stretching out from her innermost self, grasping that which was presented and being led into the café.

Over full Englishes and a pot of tea, morning drifted into afternoon. The sky above was a strange mottling of weather and seasons underneath which Max and Sophie enjoyed themselves, trying to make the best of it. Both knew the other had to return to their lives and to continue sorting through the rubble, but from this outcrop they were able to forget about it. Belinda must have been a powerful woman, Max mused to himself as he watched Sophie's uncontested airs. The next week meant moving, wholeheartedly, back into his life, something this acceptance allowed. Sophie, on the other hand, saw the rope that Max clung to blindly pass through him and was relaxed by his trajectory. She would head home tomorrow after seeing her kindly host this evening and wondered what the boys would be like now that they'd had a couple of days alone.

Chapter 32

Darkness fell and the weather closed in that Monday evening, for both Max and Sophie, as each sat alone in their respective bedrooms. The sun's glare had gone with the season, and after the overexposure of the past few months, each was left with the worlds they now existed in, unable to return, bowing under the weight of their duty to the future. A certain placidity reigned, however, and both could see the other living out the consequences.

What had, for so long, been within was now without, and it armoured them against the chaos they each had to walk through to get home. Both could see themselves in themselves, finally, and as they stood in front of their mirrors they saw a body that spoke to a mind that spoke to a soul, all looking back, through each other, returning the gaze. There was nothing to say to the other; each could see the future speaking back to the past as much as the past arranged forward the bounded future. Each had a life within a life, their own, each the centre of their own paradox and inside the eye of the storm. They inched forward as each day fell from the calendar.

*

Max awoke at six on Friday, the morning of his shoot. It was located in the Surrey Hills and a little after seven he jammed the gear stick forward, the ridiculousness of everything weighing on his mind. The traffic dawdled, stopping and starting its way to the M25 and the drivers gave each other commiserating nods. By the year, it seemed, trunk roads like these were becoming further clogged, sending traffic down the rat-runs, spilling the traffic all over the city and bringing everything to a grinding halt. Max ruefully thanked the Lord that the weather had cooled down as he absentmindedly smoked out of the driver's window. He thought that cycle lanes were the cause of this: a good had been determined and it had been applied everywhere it could be—the dim-witted pricks. A universal good dislocated from any time or place. It was an attempt at the transcendent. Humans doing God's work and the rationalisation of the irrational taken to its logical conclusion. The sweeping, granular, unwanted imposition of the dark upon the light.

Eventually he emerged from the morass, and after cruising along the M25, Max finally pulled into the National Park, parked up and dropped into the furore of the shoot. A small encampment had been set up at the end of the box canyon in which the scene would be shot, and it was nothing if not a flourishing boomtown. A harassed woman with a high and tight ponytail charged up to him, clipboard in hand, and on finding out he was a cameraman told him where to set up and rushed off, leaving Max tripod in hand and half inside the van. Once he'd emerged and found himself alone Max watched the actors hurry back and forth between rounds of makeup and the directions of various officials:

"So absurdly well planned, a veritable doll's house," Max thought to himself.

*

"*Ahriman* must fit in somewhere," Max muttered to himself, unable to quite pull the strings together. The daemon's horror lurked. It struck Max that he hadn't killed it per se. Instead, the thing had left him behind. Max had transcended beyond him—he had literally removed that 'monkey' from his back. This astounded him given the physicality of their struggle and indeed the physical deprivation of his body during that time. He had fought and fought for nothing but more fighting, only to surrender to a deeper defence. He had abandoned the redoubt to defend the keep, and only then had he won—and only in the sense that providence had given him something to split the drag.

"And so I am in love with Sophie," Max said to himself.

The words fell flat from his wavering lips and he couldn't help but shake his head a little. But he thought of that dancing child and the sudden calmness he felt with that anchoring his gaze.

"Surely I can't want one without the other," he asked the air, but his train of thought was interrupted by the bell signalling the end of lunch break, and he rose to return to the set.

The day passed uneventfully and the shoot was quick to pack up, so he left on time and drove back to London. The traffic was awful, agitating, and heavy-footed. He forwarded the van in lurches, his hands squeaking, millimetre by millimetre, over the tacky rubber wheel burning his palms.

Suddenly, Max felt those familiar cold claws on his shoulders and that hot smoky breath on the back of his neck. *Ahriman*'s laugh shivered into his ears and Max immediately smashed himself back against the seat. Of course, the daemon dodged and sat on Max's lap, dragging his head down and his gaze away from the road. Max launched himself out of the door and into the traffic standstill taking his tormentor with him. He threw him back at the side of the van and glared at the malformed wretch, now smaller but equally abominable, in front of him.

Drivers looked out their windows at the ruckus forming. Max picked up the squib and carried it to the roadside, hopping the barrier and trudging into the woods, while the shit bit and scratched him manically. In front of him, the woodland thickened, promising a clearing further on and Max slowed to a stop in front of it. It was inviting, the knarled trunks he'd have to drag *Ahriman* through before being rid of him, but it seemed somehow inappropriate. He turned back to the road and saw the traffic shuffle forward in his absence.

"But no," he looked back down at the wretch in his clasping arms and stared deep into its fearsome, mocking eyes.

"You fucking bastard," he growled,

"You'll never be rid of me you know," the daemon eyed him warmly, "I'll always be waiting in the wings for a forgotten line or a failed prompt. All those grandiose visions you have, I'm in them, I am them, you just can't see it because you haven't sat with me long enough. But you will and you'll see, I'm all of you." With that *Ahriman* settled on Max with a lurid grin.

At this Max threw his tormentor to the ground and stamped on its windpipe, crushing it with all his weight. The creature croaked and gurgled under his left foot and its eyes popped out under the strain. Max pivoted. He released Ahriman for long enough to pick up a dense limestone rock and steady himself. Once he'd got a hold of it he straightened up and dug his toes even harder into the wretch's neck, forcing all his weight onto his victim. Just as he felt the rupturing of tendons he jumped up off his left foot, and brought the rock crashing down on the figure of his daemon with both hands. Max landed astride *Ahriman* with the rock nestled between his legs. He stood up and looked at his work. The rock had landed square on *Ahriman*'s sternum and broken all its ribs under its weight. It was now swaddled by layers of ruptured organs in the cot like structure of its half shorn ribs. Now fully popped out, *Ahriman*'s eyes lay a couple of inches from his skull attached by the thinnest filament of tissue. Its arms and legs were splayed out and its head jutted askew. The whole picture was somewhat sacrificial and Max sucked the daemon's blood off the tips of his fingers as he stared down at the ugly remnants of his haunter.

Max could see the traffic budge further and horns were blaring at his stationary van so he set off back to the road looking back at the copse as he went. He didn't know what was there, but he knew it wasn't for him. Whatever it was it spoke to a part of him that, though it had existed, had been necessarily subordinated at Ahriman's return.

'Surrendering to win' was a lovely phrase he thought, but a phrase from the world from which *Ahriman* and the like came, not quite enough for this one.

Chapter 33

The next morning Max woke, again at six, and again got into his van to drive out to the M25. A little bleary-eyed, he'd fallen straight asleep the previous evening. He tapped in the location, another scene somewhere northwest of London and he picked his way through the light Saturday morning traffic.

Hunched over the steering wheel, against the shoots of sun blinding him intermittently, he ground the gearstick home to apoplectic traffic lights. It was only when Max was finally cruising along the M25 that he began to play around with Maps and scope out the location.

It was past Reading and deep in the North Wessex Downs, and with that a premonition descended.

His late-night run with the body of Matthew had been in that direction and here he was, being forced to retrace his steps. He looked in each of his mirrors and out behind him in case he was being followed. Paranoia satisfied, at least momentarily, Max floored his foot and sped towards his destination.

Soon he had reached the waste ground they were shooting on and continuing at a breakneck speed Max maniacally unloaded his gear, swearing as he did so. The production crew gathered around him initially but assuming him to be in full control left him to it. Max set up quickly and, being early, began stalking the set, angrily asking others what they were doing. This new ferocity sped up everyone else's preparations, and half an hour before the official start all were ready. In this fervour all panicked and looked to Max for leadership, assuming he was the director. Given, of course, that he wasn't and that the person in question must be on their way, a slither of realisation entered Max's mind but was unwilling to walk back down on himself.

They all hankered around him, the lot of them, and waited for his orders. When the models arrived, Max began putting them in positions, ranting madly about autumnal leaves. Cameras were set up and he took shot after shot hammering away as he barked out orders to his thralls.

The parade went on for half an hour until nine on the dot at which point the final arrival's confused shouting was heard, only to be immediately drowned out by the whine of police sirens. Max turned to see a bespectacled man, with a beard and closely cropped messy hair, step out of a large Mercedes. He was clad in a blazer too tight for his podge and a pair of bland, rolled up chinos. He was screaming. The ensuing expletives were short-lived, however, as a police car pulled up next to him and two officers jumped out and ran towards Max. One was white, short and hairy and the other was black, tall and shiny, and together they closed in. The familiar faces of Officers Richardson and N'kimbo were now against the familiar backdrop of mottled hedges and wild grass. Suddenly realising something was amiss, Max's newly created troupe dispersed with gossiping confusion and minced their way back to their respective stations. Ensconced within their materials of trade they looked like a group of judges watching an open court. Max stepped back into the set with his hands up and his eyes fixed on the police officers.

"Stop where you are, keep your hands up, and put them behind your head," yelled N'kimbo.

Overwhelmed, Max crumpled to the ground with his head bent in obsequious submission to the approaching officers. They charged towards him each grabbing an arm and manhandling him back up to handcuff his swaying figure. The triplet stood and looked around. Max with a darkening expression at his realisation and the officers with beaming grins at their success and. Leading him to their BMW, they propped him up against its boot. Looking up, behind the two policemen, Max could see the hedgerow and the bog where his crime was concealed. A body preserved by his slapdashery waiting to be exhumed. It was the beginning of the end, he was sure, and he wondered whether the officers knew of the prize that lay buried only a hundred metres behind them.

"What a surprise it is to see you here Max," Richardson remarked gleefully, "Bit of bad luck really, but we found you either way. No one likes traffic!" He nodded to a balmy N'kimbo, "We certainly weren't too excited to have to pick up the shift, but now you've come along and brightened such a glum day"!

He gestured to the overcast sky and let providence settle between them.

"You really are a Policeman's case you know, Max, you bounce from hunch to hunch until eventually you've got them where you want them."

N'kimbo, who'd busied himself with the processes, had returned sheathing his radio and waited to wade in.

"What were you doing driving so fast for, Max? You were caught on the speed cameras," Richardson asked.

"F-for the shoot," Max stammered.

"By the sounds of this man, I'd say it wasn't supposed to have started yet," replied Richardson.

"Max, what the fuck do you think you were doing," the director cut in. "It's not your fucking set, you're the fucking cameraman."

At this N'kimbo, to both Max and Richardson's relief, grabbed the slack shouldered windbag and walked him backwards out of the confrontation.

"Look, I just wanted to be here early, I was worried about being late and I gunned it," Max shook violently as he said this.

"Late to the shoot or late to here?" Richardson gestured even more expansively this time.

"I don't know what the fuck you're talking about," Max shouted! His voice was hoarse and tears flew away from his reddened eyes as he thrust from left to right.

"So there's nothing here that might scare you? Nothing that you might have been scared of someone trampling on or finding underfoot?" Richardson pushed. "Nothing you might have only remembered was here" he drew out the field's boundaries, "When you checked the location of the shoot this morning? It's been a hectic few months for you— we'd know, we've been watching,"

"I don't know what you're talking about. I have no idea what you are talking about," Max screamed and kicked the police car with the heel of his shoe as tears streamed down his face.

"Busy, busy, you've had all sorts going on haven't you, Max? But you haven't worked much in that time have you, not really until now if we're honest. Maybe one or two jobs, but I reckon this is you getting back into the swing of things, isn't it? And I bet you were so concerned with that need to be on the ball, to be moving and to be working, that you hadn't even bothered to check exactly where you were going until this morning, ain't that right?"

Richardson had advanced a couple of steps and twisted himself slightly so he could peer up right into Max's averted eyes.

"Max it's all over, you've fallen right into our lap. We know why you're here, we know you were so rattled when you hit the M25 that you had to race along an open road. And we know why you're running around like a maniac. We know where Matt's buried."

Max raised his eyes to meet Richardson's and saw the cold resolution of manifest destiny shine up from his pale stubbly face. Looking deeper, he thought he saw a glimmer of sympathy turning in the police officer's dark eyes, the lady in the lake, Britannia. She spoke to him and he felt his guts unwind, his forehead cleared and his lips parted. She invited his crime out of him—it was a daemon begging to be excised and he saw himself falling into the policeman's arms…

"Right Max, there's a very serious accusation here," N'kimbo interrupted, "I'd like to ask you a few questions."

Richardson wrenched around, furious, unaware his senior had returned from placating the director. In this vacuum Max regained himself and tripped forwards into N'kimbo's diplomatic arms, pleading,

"Whatever it is, it's a job for Mr Valentine," he spluttered, "Take me to the station."

At this Richardson stepped towards N'kimbo, absolutely apoplectic with rage, but the clammy figure of the director got between them before the junior officer could do anything.

"Officers charge this man with trespassing and misusing equipment! He's signed contracts, he's liable"!

He waved his iPhone like a condom at a pregnant lady yelling enough to make the doctor miss the birth. N'kimbo shoved the director back where he came from and, assured by his momentum, roughly pushed the grateful Max around to the BMWs backdoor.

"He was going to confess N'kimbo"!

The enraged Richardson pulled his fellow around leaving Max leant against the car.

"It'll all come out in the wash Officer," N'kimbo retorted, "Let's not inconvenience the crew any further. All this can be conducted back at the station."

"Your belligerence!" Richardson erupted," It's unbelievable. You'll let him get away with it because of what? Because I've run this instead of you, is that it?" Richardson's emotions, unused to their raw expression, flooded far past his reason.

"So you admit it!" accused N'kimbo, "You've been taking this your own way, to satisfy your own means, and now you're angry that your senior officer is dragging it back on course? That says enough about you detective—you'll be dealing with a write-up when we're back in Charing Cross!"

*

What followed next can only be described as an utter breakdown in police discipline, and unfortunately for those involved it ended up on every front page the next morning. It ran from there to pages three and four and from the first segment of an evening to a secondary story. Over the next month it went from a viral explosion to a running gag. In that time the full force of the British journalistic establishment was brought to bear on it, and by mid-October the subjects had been sliced up and taped back together so often that they resembled some godforsaken collage. Those involved, of course, being limited to the two policemen.

Chapter 34

The funeral began at eleven. The family arrived at ten and they wandered about the gravel car park each consumed in mourning. The older two led the younger two around the perimeter. Their slow, trudging laps left Alastair standing, vacant, in the centre. Their father was far away, staring into the distance and alone.

The church was only a short walk away and there Vicar Powell would be completing the final preparations for the service.

It all felt so pathetic.

It was as if they were pacing, unawares, around the rehearsal room for a play they didn't know they were performing.

And still, her father stood, looking out to somewhere. Sophie couldn't imagine he'd ever felt more alone. Thirty-five years of marriage were now beginning to extract their price and his lone rotund form was bereft, forever, of its enwrapping comfort. He was a figurehead, driven towards his final sanctuary, supported by his issue.

It had been decided that the children would be pallbearers, along with two volunteers from the funeral home, and so as Vicar Powell emerged from the church they formed up and chose a position.

"Hello everyone," Powell began sweetly, "Shall we begin?" she turned and gestured to the church.

The family filed along behind her and she took them to the font where she explained the finalised proceedings. Each family member received a paper booklet outlining their roles and was pointed towards their respective readings. Finally, Alastair was comforted. Each child had been assigned a Biblical extract and Alastair the eulogy, and the group broke up into themselves examining their charges. Vicar Powell took this opportunity to pull Sophie aside,

"I hope our talk helped somewhat Sophie, I appreciate it wasn't quite as conclusive as it might have been but please consider me a source of strength in this difficult time."

Her grip on Sophie's elbow relaxed and Sophie returned her sympathetic glance with one of her own,

"Thank you, it did … Now if you don't mind I'd better start greeting the guests," she replied simply.

And with that everything began. Over the next half an hour the church filled with cousins, aunts; uncles, family friends, and locals. The latter abated the ceremonial a little, under the force of the people, gratifying Sophie. Eventually the service began, the guests sat in their pews and Vicar Powell took her place in the pulpit.

"Ladies and gentlemen, thank you for joining us here on this most tragic day…"

*

Finally, everyone started to file out for the wake and the family were left to bear the coffin to its final resting place. Alastair followed the procession and together they walked to a plot in a secluded corner of the graveyard. There, under a young oak, the stone wall gave way revealing the tumbling valleys behind. Once at the grave the children were replaced by four others so they could stand with their father to watch their mother being lowered into her final resting place. Finally, Vicar Powell gave Belinda her last rite and the family stood in silence.

By the time they'd arrived at the wake the booze was flowing and the condolences came around once again. Their uncle Giles had already managed to get himself plastered and was loudly telling stories of how he and his sister had played as children, how they'd romped around the fields and then the pubs and then the city and then back to the fields once again. A little shallow some might say, betraying more than necessary about everyone involved. Yet unfortunately he kept going. After all, he had a lifetime of B-roll for his awkward audience, and was tarnishing his sister's image with every anecdote. The highlights were yet to begin, however, some of their local friends pulled Sophie aside and told cheeky stories of how her pre, mid, and postnatal mother had stolen hours away with them over a bottle or two only to be wound in by her concerned father. It was all so anodyne. Giles took it upon himself to end the torment by reintroducing his own, and recalled the crowd for another speech.

"Belinda really was pretty wild," he chortled drunkenly, spitting red wine all over a luckless child. "On one occasion, oh there was one occasion," he swayed and shook his forefinger, "When, she beheaded a chicken with a rusted butter knife!" The chatter fell silent. Unfortunately, Giles had his eyes closed and his ears full. "She found it in the grass, the knife I mean, and grabbed a nearby chicken and sawed its head off one evening after we'd got back from the pub. The damn thing squawked awfully until she'd finally beheaded it. She kept it for a bit I think, or maybe she threw it away, it was all such a long time ago."

Chapter 35

Max walked quickly towards Eros, a newspaper under his arm, looking for Sophie. It was the Thursday after their respective ordeals (the fight and the funeral) and she was someone amongst the masses. Max peeled his belle out of the crowd and they walked up into Soho. It was late afternoon and the world was strange—where was the routine? Tired and tried the narrow streets of Soho surrounded them as they walked. Max had completed his job on Sunday as planned and had largely spent the days since with his parents of all people. It had been a strange reunion; they were worlds apart now, and he looked back into their life as if it were a fishbowl. They had worked to release themselves from obligation which gave their protestations about the state of the nation a hollow shrillness. Max had felt little warmth over those few days and the stay had acted less as a restorative and more as a clarifier. Sophie, for herself, had remained at home with her family and was now down until Sunday looking for work.

The pair settled in a pub on the corner of two streets and sat at the window watching the pedestrians walk by. It was overhung with memorabilia and portraits and attracted a diverse crowd of suited fish, checked shirts, greasy metrosexuals, and an assorted smattering of young people—the native diaspora. Despite this Max felt lonesome. It wasn't so much the episode with his parents itself, but rather that it had proved what was already the case. He was a collection of his self-inflicted scars and only he could line them up like steps to his future. Officers Richardson and N'kimbo's fight had lost them the case by Monday, and Max had been summoned to Charing Cross on the same day. To his surprise, Valentine hadn't been there and instead Max was brought into an empty office at the end of a musty corridor and told that the case against him had been dropped. And with that, he had been told to get on his way—that was the end of it. There had been no trace of the case in the media coverage and instead the focus had been on quotas within the Met. The shallowness of the reporting had astounded many, and comments had run to that conclusion. But it made no difference to the narrative and the punch-up had been turned into a flooring on which various governmental hopefuls began vying for their own self-prophesied ascendancy. There had been no mention of Valentine, nor was much depth given to either professional career up to that point.

Max had thought to call his impromptu lawyer and thank him for all his help with the interviews. They had had a brief conversation in which the subject of what he would do now he was retired was carefully avoided by both. He was, however, sanguine about the prospects of those junior to him and assumed that Richardson had kept his job. If anything Max thought, it was Valentine and Richardson who would stay in touch. The lawyer did, however, leave Max with some advice,

"Whatever the hell you do lad never go back to that damn field ever again. It's verboten from now on, you might as well cut it out of the map. It wasn't your day to go down, that much is clear, but don't ever give it another chance to get purchase in that sloppy little head of yours. You're a man now and you'd best take these things seriously."

A knowing tone rang through this gravitas weighed statement and Max gulped it down taking deep heed. He thanked Valentine again and hung up to the view of the morning's sun gracing Tuesday's rooftops. The field, Matthew and *Ahriman* folded up behind him, but out in front, through the curtains, a vale was beheld and beckoned him.

Now in the pub, Max had laid the newspaper out between him and Sophie with amusement at the headline, 'Busting Coppers Dragged to Trial.' There was talk of what would happen to them, where they'd go and how they'd be treated once their grimacing mug shots had been splattered around. Richardson had managed to communicate his working-class lilt through his eyes, and this had caused some fantastical speculation amongst the journos. N'kimbo was as impassive as ever which produced as much ire amongst a different camp. The whole episode reeked of self-propulsion and this would no doubt drag the story who knows where. It was already so divorced from the truth that Max and Sophie managed to have an entire conversation about it without even mentioning Max's relation to them. When they eventually did reach the topic of the case, Max explained that the Police had simply moved on and it seemed to him that they had been so bereft of evidence they had been searching just to say that they were searching. This satisfied Sophie enough and the matter was dropped.

Sophie, for her part, had been looking for a job—rather unsuccessfully thus far. She had, of course, pursued various options spun off from her previous post, but to little avail.

Her heart wasn't in it and it weighed increasingly heavily on her as she tapped her way through the LinkedIn filtering. This uncomfortability seemed a newly discovered compass that tore at her guts when her body was off-tack. It was a burden as much as a gift, though she was yet to receive it in its positive form. Eventually, she brought her lack of inspiration to the dinner table only to receive a few haphazard suggestions in their rough effort to comfort her in her indecision. The dining room had been discontinued as a workspace and returned to normal and she spent most days lounging between there and the sitting room picking up wherever she'd left off with a family member when they walked by. It was a slow life and she led from the soul. It bore her around the land on a consistent swell and occasionally deposited her, curled-up reading, on the sofa. Alastair continued his pottering but spent more time sitting, and watched his family address the needs of the house, relaxed now that the reins were in their hands. He loved hearing Sophie's ideas about what she might do and enjoyed seeing her think out the world she would be walking back into.

The next day Sophie said her goodbyes to everyone and Arthur gave her a lift to the station. They roared through the country lanes sweeping past open fields and their wild gorse divisions. Arthur was ebullient and explained his plans for their backfields. The great unsaid was left in the dust for this slice of time. He pulled up to the station and they sat in the car together. Arthur removed a leather pouch from the glovebox and placed it on his lap. He opened it and removed Sophie's jack and presented it to her.

"You really must have been sure of yourself to get us to pass around a feeling stick"!

"It's not a bloody feeling stick," she replied, exasperated.

"I know," pacified Arthur, "I think I'm beginning to understand it. We're all a little more bound together with that wand being waved among us."

Sophie had sat on the train overwhelmed at her brother's gratitude, and thought of her mother. She looked down on Sophie from far above and as Sophie gazed up at her she saw an Icon before her. She thought about what Giles had said about their childhood and wondered what Belinda had borne into motherhood. Sophie would never know, and now it didn't matter. The gestures and deficiencies had fizzled away and all that was left was the comfort of the ideal and all the dimensionality that gave. An ever mother, she now topped the tree as its latest branch and angled out in arching elegance. Sophie wondered when she would join her and what a grove they'd have to look back on together. This was enough, Sophie supposed, she had done enough to get through and had been given enough to sustain her. She wasn't anchored by it and she wasn't underweight because of it. Still in balance, she continued her pirouetting on the tones of her soul.

*

Together Max and Sophie now sat with that ridiculous newspaper between them and wondered how it would all end. The drinks sat at opposite corners of the paper and it seemed as though the pieces had fallen into place.

"What are you going to do now?" they asked each other in unison.

Max fingered the paper a little awkwardly, pursing his lips at the question while Sophie sat in a chaste serenity slamming all the bubbling within her hard down inside her. There was no game of gazes to play, yet they play they did, making coquettish forays into the other's psyche. Finally, Max pulled himself up and sat himself back against the wall and began,

"I've gotta get out of what I'm doing too, I think," Sophie nodded slowly, "Give up the flat and move is what I've been thinking,"

"Ha, well I'm back at home for the foreseeable," she giggled,

"Ah…," Max admitted. The conversation lulled once again. "So what about us then," Max said with a braced off-handedness.

"What about us?" Sophie teasingly replied. Max sighed to himself and cradling his fear leaned in,

"Well, I think we should keep seeing each other. It's not often you meet someone and manage to weather a murder investigation together!" His jocular tone set Sophie off laughing and she breathlessly replied,

"Why yes I suppose we've rather jumped the gun to marital problems, really."

"Well yes … at least some might say," Max continued, his humour giving way to sincerity,

"You and I would be great. Anyway, I'd like to make good on you, my guiding light, for bearing me through the last few months."

"Oh, Prince charming how you win me!," Sophie cut in as she fluttered her eyelashes and weighed her words with a mocking, sultry tone and she grabbed her tits and threw her head back and around just for good measure.

"Oh," Max coughed, exasperated, "I thought I already had." The mention shot them both back to that evening and Sophie's eyes and lips pursed at the memory.

"You know, I think I know what I want to do next," she said tangentially, "I'd like to become a writer, you know it'd be fun, it'd be mine." At this, she leaned back and set Max with a deceptive gaze. There was a flash of expectancy in her pupils and she knew their relationship ultimately, whatever it may be, would rest on the outcome of this statement. Max eyed her back and thought about what their dreams would mean so tightly intertwined.

"I've been thinking about going it alone too, in my own way," he nodded with a hint of reticence, "I've got the expertise, access to the kit and, well, finally the space to build in. The walls have been erected, I know where I am. I suppose I'd like to see where it takes me too. Sophie nodded silently. She nudged the newspaper over to him and bit her lip,

"You still carry this you know, whatever happened in those interviews still weighs on you and you'll spend however long you need to disabusing yourself of whatever you've come to believe in lieu of it being lifted. It might last a lifetime, for all I know, but it's your charge to keep shouldering it until it ceases to exist."

"You're more right than you could ever know," Max said sombrely, "I've come to know this just as you've described it but I came to know it before, as only I, the subject of it all, can. The more familiar I become with this particular paradox the more I realise that what actually matters is that I keep a tight grip on it and drive ever forward. You're right to as much the same extent as I am and the depth of each of our truths can only really be known to each of us exclusively. But none of that matters. Knowing, knowing anything, only matters if it deepens the realisation that action is all that can break the ever-complexifying impasse. Action is all.

All you've told me is the next level of depth I need to continue on my current course, to live the decision I made however long ago."

"Aren't we just a span of decisions made waiting for the splattering of a slip?" Max blushed at this and hung his chin to his chest.

He looked up through hooded eyes to the woman before him and lay awash within her beauty. Sophie was enchanted by the fathoming earnestness that the man opposite her marshalled under his leadership and she relaxed into his safety.

Max reached a hand over the table and grasped one of Sophie's.

"There'll always be something between us I'm sure, a string that vibrates at your call and jerks me back around to you. And in a sense there's nothing I'd rather do than sign off here and walk out that door with you but I just don't think I can. I so want to, but I can finally feel myself pulled along by that which has us all in our own ways whether we accept it or not. I've never been less conscious of myself and yet I've probably been more unmistakably singular as I am now. At this Sophie's eyes glistened and she smiled and nodded in painful agreement. "And I think the same is true for you too. I don't know who you are now your mother's gone but I can see you're aware of your binding by it. Sophie nodded. "I'm beginning to become the woman I was meant to be,"

Nodding again, this time to herself, "One day you'll see her, but I'm touched you know she's there. Whatever else," she snorted, "This is certainly real and we're certainly alive. I don't think I've felt more like I know I should before; and I know I'm going to walk out that door without you, just wishing we could stay seated and take the picture 'to show how young we were back then'."

At this, they fell silent. They swam in each other's features and dived down to the depths of their soul.

"I don't even get to say you're the best thing that never happened to me and thank God." At this, Max rose and put on his jacket. He turned to leave and giving Sophie one last look, went out through the double doors.

Later Sophie collected her things and got up, she turned and carefully touched the table with her forefingers and then went to leave. She saw Max's figure walking away down the left-hand road and turned the opposite way. They parted like this, along the hands of a clock, only as far away as time would let them, and only for as long as their tides drove them apart. It was then, of course, that London Bridge Fell.